About the Author

Mark began his writing career in the business world. In 2005, he wrote *Flight of the Mayflower* that attracted excellent critical and reader reviews. In 2019, Mark wrote two books back-to-back, including *Born in a Storm*. After travelling the world and residing in three countries, Mark now lives with his wife of thirty years in a leafy suburb of Brisbane, Australia.

Born in a Storm

Mark Carew

Born in a Storm

Vanguard Press

A CIP catalogue record for this title is
available from the British Library.

ISBN 978 1 83794 110 0

Vanguard Press is an imprint of
Pegasus Elliot Mackenzie Publishers Ltd.
www.pegasuspublishers.com

First Published in 2024

Vanguard Press
Sheraton House Castle Park
Cambridge England

Printed & Bound in Great Britain

To Kimberley

November 1987

The nondescript man left his home in Westphalia, Maryland, allowing himself plenty of time to make his speaking engagement at the Washington National Press Club.

His route followed the I-495 Capital Beltway, through the turnpike, then west up Pennsylvania Avenue.

He was a sober fellow, yet allowed himself a small smile as he enjoyed the free-flowing traffic conditions. He surmised most commuters had reached their work destination for the day.

Driving without the need to navigate or battle traffic, the man practiced his upcoming speech. Today was the day the whole world would change, and humankind's greatest threat would be halted in its tracks, and with luck, be reversed.

What he failed to notice was the large black SUV weaving through traffic behind him. He also failed to acknowledge an interstate truck intent on holding its position to his left.

It was late spring, and the man enjoyed the seasonal warmth. He loved the bright morning colours and could see the city buildings emerging from the morning haze.

He turned on the radio, just in time for Mantovani and his orchestra to play Charmaine. He reached down and turned the volume up, filling his car with the soft, relaxing sound.

As the music soothed his world, the black SUV moved up to his right. He was now sandwiched between the SUV and the truck.

In one choreographed motion, the truck edged back a fraction, while the SUV rammed the front end of the man's car. The impact was sudden and brutal, and spun him directly into the path of the truck.

The man's car was thrown down the road like a child's toy rolling; wheels to roof, over and over, many times before it finally stopped, landing on its wheels.

The SUV also stopped, and the driver ran toward the man's car carrying a heavy pinch bar.

He attempted to open the driver's side door, but as expected, it was jammed. It took several heaves with the pinch bar to open it. Still in his seat, the man was conscious and trying to speak.

The driver held his head and in one practiced move, snapped the man's neck. He reached over the man's body to find a briefcase. He opened it and scanned the cover of a document titled: 'Unlocking Zero Point Energy — the Clean Energy Solution.'

He took the document and returned to the SUV. Ten seconds later, he was absorbed by the Washington traffic.

2007 — USS Ronald Regan (CVN 76)

Somewhere off the Southern Californian coast.

Four F/A-18 Super Hornets sat crouched on the flight deck of the mighty carrier with their engines howling.

The massive ship pitched lightly in the moderate seas, as Lieutenant Mackenzie James felt a river of sweat run down his back.

He was about to experience sixty-six thousand pounds of pilot and plane accelerate from zero to one hundred and sixty-five knots in three seconds. One piece of equipment failure or incorrect flight setting, and he would bounce off the deck, into the sea. Stranded and helpless before the unstoppable bulk of the one hundred thousand ton aircraft carrier moving at over thirty knots.

His eyes scanned his instrument screen. Fuel, electrical, oxygen, hydraulics, flaps, weapons, and radios. All were in the green.

His head on swivel, Mack watched his aircraft handler-chief lead him through an array of flight surface tests.

Mack's flight of four F-18s was designated 'Duster'. The flight leader was Duster One. Mack was his wingman, designated Duster Two. The second flight element was Duster Three and Four.

The F-18s were being launched from the carrier on two sperate launch ramps. The launch lamp was lit, and the clock was running.

As an early teen growing up in New York City, Mackenzie James was far from an "A" level student. His heart was drawn more toward pretty girls and violent sport.

Not particularly tall, or handsome, his blessing was his fearlessness. He fought bullies larger than himself and pursued girls out of his league. His aggression won him most fights, and on a sliding scale, he scored with semi-predictable success with the girls.

His parents and teachers, however, thought him more a little shit. The term most often used was 'precocious little shit'. A boy with huge potential and very little motivation in committing himself to assigned lessons.

That all changed one sunny morning in September 2001.

Mack was at school where his first class for the day had begun. Minutes later, the school headmaster burst in and asked his teacher to follow him. The headmaster, who on any other day resembled the terminator, sent back in time to whip schoolboys, looked nervous and rattled.

The students were stunned. What had Mrs Cline done? Theories formed immediately, not all of them decent.

Mack's curiosity got the better of him, and as was his nature, he went to investigate. He walked past the teacher's lounge where the entire teaching staff was watching a TV screen. Mack walked in and was immediately ignored. He edged closer until he could see the screen.

There he saw smoke pouring out from one of the World Trade Towers, with a caption announcing a plane had hit it. As he watched, a second large passenger liner flew directly into the South Tower.

His teachers gave wails of shock and young Mack felt instantly sick. He knew this was no coincidence; something was terribly wrong.

His teacher's words confirmed his fears; America was under attack.

In the following days, young Mack's shock and fear turned to rage. His America, his city, was attacked by terrorists and thousands of people were dead.

The then sixteen-year-old Mackenzie James made a vow. He would kill the bastards who helped make this happen, then kill all the bastards who might do it again.

Mack dropped his extracurricular activities and hit the books. He requested tutors for math and science, where his parents were delighted to help the boy.

Within a year Mack's grades were at "A" levels.

Just before his eighteenth birthday, Mack took the SATs and earned a 1600 score. His efforts were enough to gain a spot in the prestigious U.S. Naval Academy, and eventually the Navy Flight School.

Mack's aptitude as a potential fighter pilot revealed itself. He had the rare 'X' factor of aggression tempered with judgement and natural ability in the cockpit. Along with his newly acquired study discipline, these qualities ensured his selection into jets.

At the age of twenty-four, after eighteen months of fighter jet training, and two certification deployments, Mack was a war-ready naval aviator.

On deck, Mack focused on the task at hand.

In one choreographed action, the aircraft handlers raced away from his F-18 and crouched to avoid the upcoming jet blast.

Launch was close.

The F-18 to his right was his flight leader. His leader gave his salute, and seconds later his jet was hurled down the flight deck into clear air.

Mack was next.

The catapult commander did his final checks from inside his on-deck launch bubble. Rear, side, front, all clear. He set the catapult pressure to maximum.

With a smart salute, Mack throttled up to full military power and did a final rapid circuit of his flight controls. The F-18 strained against the launch block.

The catapult officer paused for a second, ensuring Mack's F-18 was at maximum power and the engines were stable.

Last check, and launch.

In a rush of released energy, his F-18 kicked Mack in the back hard and hurled him down the three hundred foot deck. With a heavy grunt, Mack sucked air back into his lungs and commenced his climb.

Repeating the dance of men and machines, the second flight element of Dusters Three and Four were launched. Everyone on the carrier was earning their pay that day.

Duster Flight formed a loose formation, racing through ten thousand feet, toward their fifty thousand feet assigned flight level.

They headed to a waypoint one hundred and fifty miles northeast of the carrier to establish a CAP, or combat air patrol.

The "Red" team, who posed as the enemy for this exercise, were armed with brand new fifth-generation Advanced Harpoon Anti-Ship missiles.

The Red Team had launched thirty minutes earlier with instructions to lose themselves in wave clutter. To fly at wave-top level, or spook the fish, as the pilots knew it.

A Northrop Grumman E-2 Hawkeye was already on station, thirty-five thousand feet above the fray. She was the eyes of the fleet, and her job was to track everything that flew in the theatre of operations. The E-2 could identify and track an almost unlimited number of targets at all ranges, bearings, and altitudes.

Today, her team was testing a radar guided anti-missile laser targeting system. The hope was this system could locate very low flying aircraft at long-range before it got into a position to fire their missiles at the American carrier.

It was a big day for the Hawkeye team. If they failed to identify and track the Red Team aircraft, many millions of dollars and thousands of man hours in development was wasted.

Airborne communications had begun.

'Duster One-Four, Hawkeye. Comms check, how copy?' Duster leader asked. Duster was the enemy kill team for this mission and Hawkeye was their eyes.

'Hawkeye, Duster One-Four. I copy.'

A few minutes later, 'Hawkeye, Duster flight. Execute in zero-five minutes. How copy?'

The exercise was to begin in five minutes.

'Copy, Hawkeye, zero-five.'

In this quiet interval, two hundred miles from the carrier, the Red Team was down to wave-top flight level, preparing to make their attack run.

'Duster One-Four, Hawkeye. Report all contacts, over.'

'Duster, your sky is clear.'

The minutes dragged on.

Mack, flying as Duster Two-Four, maintained his position five feet behind and a little to the right of his leader.

The second element, Duster Three and Four, were positioned high and close to protect the first two fighters. When combat is met, they would be called upon to perform tactical manoeuvres for air superiority.

All flight communications were linked between the four Duster F-18s. Hawkeye maintained tactical command, while strategic mission command was reserved for the Task Force Admiral based on the carrier.

'What the fuck is that!' Duster One-Four yelled suddenly. Group silence.

'Hawkeye, Duster, say again?'

'Hawkeye, do you have a target up here with us?'

At that moment Mackenzie James saw what his flight leader was looking at. A round-edged luminous oblong, a thousand yards directly ahead.

'Duster Two, do you have a visual on the bogy?' Duster leader asked.

Mack touched his mic. 'Affirm. I see it.'

This was very wrong. No aircraft targets were on the Hawkeye scope, and the Red Team was some one hundred and fifty miles to the east, almost fifty thousand feet below them.

Duster leader made a formal declaration of the situation.

'Duster One-Four, Hawkeye. I have a visual on a northern bogy. Range one thousand yards, bearing zero degrees from my heading. My wingman has confirmed visual. I am going to radar.'

Duster One-Four activated and scanned his radar. Nothing.

'Duster One-Four to all Duster aircraft. Activate radar and report.'

'Duster Two, No radar, visual only.'

'Duster Three, only visual.'

'Four, visual.'

'Duster One-Four, Hawkeye. My bogy is it at my twelve o'clock. He's matching my course and speed. He's a luminous, ah, oblong-looking craft. It looks like some kind of flying tic tac. I'm locking him up on my thermal camera now. Ah, okay, I've got him locked. Oh God! What the hell is this thing.'

'Hawkeye, Duster One-Four. We are tracking your bogy now. He just appeared on the screen.'

'Copy, Hawkeye. I can't see any flight surfaces. Thermal shows no heat plume and he's doing some four hundred knots against the wind.'

'Duster, can you estimate its size?'

'I estimate, ah, maybe thirty feet long and twelve feet across. Ah, can't be sure. Has blurry edges. Repeat, I see no wings, no stabilizers of any kind. Confirming, he has no heat signature at all!'

Silence.

'Hawkeye! Wait one! Bogy is manoeuvring. He's turning! He's coming straight at me!'

The tension in his voice was clear to all listening.

'Duster Three and Four, break high and right! Come in around behind this guy!'

'Copy, One.' The two trailing F-18s broke away and began their climb with afterburners lit.

'Duster Two, spread formation…'

Too late, the luminous craft was on top of them, flashing through the narrow space between Duster 1 and 2 at eight hundred knots closure.

Mack watched the white oblong as it slid by.

'Oh, fuck me,' Mack intoned.

'Duster Two, don't lose visual!'

'I have him. He's looping around, coming back on our six!'

'Break high, I'll go low. Let's scissor the bastard! At the top of your turn come down on his six.'

The fighters hit the power and performed the manoeuvre. The bogy was gone.

'What the fuck! Hawkeye, Hawkeye, Duster One-Four, we have a hostile bogy. I'm arming sidewinders. Do I have permission to fire?'

Silence.

'Wait one! There he is! Oh shit! He's now at one mile. Seems to be in a hover! How is this possible?'

Silence

'Hawkeye, Hawkeye! I am attempting sidewinder missile lock, ah, can't seem to engage. Sidewinders can't get a heat lock! Oh shit! My weapons are dead. I'm going to guns. All Duster aircraft, form on me for a gun attack on target.'

'Copy, One,' they answered in turn.

'Bogy is now matching my speed. Flying away on bearing zero degrees, still on my nose. I can still get a long-range shot. Gun safety off.'

At that moment a new voice came over comms.

'Base-Plate (The carrier), Duster aircraft. Command override, repeat, command override. DO NOT engage the bogy! Copy my last.'

Silence.

19

'Duster One-Four, Base-Plate. We copy. Do not engage.'

Duster One-Four was disappointed, yet not a little relieved. His initial instinct to kill the intruding hostile bogy was normal, based on years of combat training. As a fighter pilot, he was a hammer, and hammers only see nails.

But he knew whatever this thing was, it was far more advanced than his own weapon system. The UAP (Unknown Aerial Phenomena) had completely outclassed his F-18.

Whatever this craft was, he knew it was playing with them. He also knew it wasn't Russian or Chinese.

'Base Plate, Duster Flight. Return to the flight deck immediately and report to flight briefing. Maintain air and ship-board silence until that time. No more chatter. That is all, how copy?"

'Duster One-Four, copy. No chatter, we are RTB (return to base).'

The Red Devil flight of Harpoon F-18s were operating on a separate frequency and had no idea what was happening. They made a textbook attack on the carrier and wondered why the CAP had not attempted an intercept.

'Red Devil One-Four, harpoons away. Sorry to say, the carrier is dead. Have a nice day.'

'Hawkeye, Red Devil One-Four. Exercise is terminated. RTB, how copy?'

'Copy, Hawkeye. We are RTB,' he said. Just another techno clusterfuck, the Devils leader mused.

Thirty minutes later, all four Duster pilots were gathered in the flight briefing room clutching mugs of steaming black coffee.

The briefing room hatchway opened, and three men stepped through, including the ship's captain and the taskforce admiral. Two more men they did not know joined them, both wearing navy uniforms with the rank of commander. They had no badges or patches.

'Regardless of what you thought you saw today, three things actually occurred,' the ship's captain began. 'One. A civilian corporate jet flew off course and entered the exercise area. Two. To avoid a collision with the civilian jet you took evasive manoeuvres. Three. Your quick thinking and actions saved the lives of the civilians onboard. This unforeseen event caused you to lose contact with the Red Flight and the exercise was scrubbed.'

The pilots viewed the man impassively. They felt numb and stupefied. The admiral stepped forward.

'You men demonstrated great maturity and judgement today. Due to your actions, no one was harmed. For that I have approved commendations for all of you, as submitted to me by your group commander, and countersigned by your captain.'

'Sir, can you tell us if the craft was one of ours?' Mack asked.

The senior officers stared at him.

'Do you have a hearing problem, Lieutenant?' the captain asked. 'Let me make this very clear; a private jet entered your air space, and that's all you saw.'

Mack knew the conversation was over.

'Yes, sir,' Mack said impassively. 'A private jet.'

The senior officers, and two unknown commanders, left the room.

'What the hell?' Mack faced his team. 'A civilian jet!'

'My advice is this; shut the fuck up,' his flight leader told him. 'That goes for all of you knuckleheads. Talk to no one on the ship. No letters home. No emails or phone calls. This did not happen, clear?'

The team nodded in silence. This was the navy, not a corporate boardroom. They were well schooled in when to speak and when to obey a direct command.

In the following days and weeks, Mack relived the experience several times. He could reach only one conclusion. The UAP flew without wings or visible signs of propulsion. It performed well beyond the capacity of his F-18 and flew under intelligent control.

The burning question in Mack's mind was, *where did it get its power, if not from burning combustible fuel?*

The Interview

'Welcome to World Live Tonight!' the announcer told the audience. 'We are filmed before a live studio audience right here in the city of London. Now here is your host, Rowland Smith!'

The audience clapped and whooped. It was nearly impossible to get tickets for this show, forcing people to line up for days. The lucky few who got in were happy and loud.

'Good evening, everyone! I'm Rowland Smith and for the very first time the world will meet Lucas Harding, the lead scientist who, along with his intrepid team, changed how the world will receive its electrical power!'

'Hello Rowland,' Lucas began. 'Thank you for having me on your show.'

'History gave us the steam engine, the industrial age, space travel, and modern medicine,' Smith told the cameras. 'Now all of humanity is about to run our homes, cars, and factories on zero emissions electricity, and it's virtually cost free!'

The studio audience roared in applause.

Smith checked his notes. 'I am reading your press release. It says in the pursuit of developing this planet-saving marvel, at the critical point of our climate catastrophe, you were threatened, pursued, and very nearly killed by the highest levels of the US Government.'

Smith paused for the audience to catch up, then continued.

'The US government placed a kill order on you and your team. You were pursued across the US, the Pacific Ocean, and all the way to South America. Your research lab was bombed and several of your colleges were killed.'

The cameras focused on Lucas Harding, who could only nod his head. Attempting to speak of the losses was not wise while the world was watching him.

'How does a journey like this begin? Perhaps from the beginning?'

'Okay, here we go...' Lucas began.

Lucas Harding's father was a man named Thomas.

Thomas was a mad keen sailor who liked to push the limits of his obsession. In his eyes, a strong breeze was an element to tame, and his boat was an instrument with which he would do the taming. Sadly, this monomaniacal tunnel vision often led to broken boats and bleeding people.

Many people who knew Thomas Harding did not know how he had survived as long as he did. Yacht clubs up and down the East coast of America had banned Thomas from match races, and few of his friends would ever sail with him.

From his front yard on the shore of Chesapeake Bay, Virginia, Tom and Lucas watched the weather building far off to the south, down Mobjack Bay.

He explained to Lucas the storm was still a good four hours away, giving them plenty of time to clear Mobjack, tack right, and run north with the wind behind them.

'We'll broad reach all the way up the Chesapeake!' Thomas told twelve-year-old Lucas.

At twelve years old, Lucas Harding was still at an age where he implicitly trusted his father and wanted nothing more than to impress him with his bravery.

He was already a seasoned sailor, having spent hundreds of hours smashing his way through angry waves in howling winds, right there next to his dad in Chesapeake. He loved the sailing and that feeling of almost rebirth after a hard day on the water.

'We'll have plenty of time to reach Tangier Island,' he told his wife.

Jan Harding knew Tangier was some twenty miles sailing to the north, up the bay, and by then, the storm would have arrived.

'You'll barely make the bay by the time it hits,' she told her husband.

'Don't worry. We'll have a great sailing angle for the northern run. I've done this a thousand times.'

She knew there was no changing her husband's mind once the sailing bug stung him.

'Come on, Lucas!' Tom said. 'Get your jacket. We're off on an adventure!'

Twenty minutes later, their Oceanis 34 motored past Crab Point and into Mobjack Bay. Tom could feel the breeze picking up and could see the clouds forming due south.

A moment of doubt plucked a chord in his mind, where Thomas Harding promptly dismissed it. *We're committed now*, he told himself.

Thomas headed the boat into the wind and gave Lucas his instructions.

'Take the helm and head due south. I'll get the sails up.'

Young Lucas loved the responsibility of piloting the boat and focused hard on maintaining his bearing.

With the boat in a good luff position, Thomas raised the mainsail and unfurled the jib.

'Port fifteen degrees!' Thomas called.

The new bearing stopped the luff, and the sails caught the breeze. At once, the boat heeled over and picked up speed.

'We're sailing, kill the motor!' Tom called to Lucas.

At once, silence filled the air. It was a magical thing to move with such grace, pushed along by the wind, sliding over the swell of the bay.

Tom close-hauled the sails, giving the Oceanis another three knots of boat speed.

As the wind picked up, they heeled to twenty degrees. Lucas trusted his father completely and knew this was all completely normal.

He loved the sensation of heeling and the random splashes of the water as the boat broke the tops of the waves.

Tom, however, was watching the storm. It was bigger than he first thought and approaching fast. He wanted to make New Point Comfort Lighthouse where he could come north and run with the weather.

But the storm had other ideas.

It was now blowing at twenty-five knots and shifting southeast, directly into their path.

Tom checked his position. He could see the Crab Point Lighthouse was still a mile off. He needed the wind to stay southerly for another twenty minutes.

Lucas could see his father was not relaxed and he began to feel a little unease. They close-hauled as best they could for another five minutes until Thomas calculated they would not clear the lighthouse.

'We've run out of water,' he told his son.

With the wind coming directly down their bearing Tom would have to commence tacking across the bay. That would be extremely time-consuming and dangerous with a young boy as his only crew.

'I'm not sure this was such a great idea!' Tom had to yell through a wind was now reaching thirty knots.

'We're going about!' he yelled. 'I want you below!'

Lucas was getting scared. Things were happening very fast and he could see his father was worried.

With Lucas safely in the cabin, Tom broached the boat across the waves and wind. He set the sails to a broad reach, fixing the sails wide with the wind behind them.

With the boat stable and racing back to home before the storm, Lucas came back on deck.

'See!' Tom told him. 'That wasn't so…'

Crack!

High in the sky, some ten miles away, two massive water-ladened clouds tumbled past each other as they raced north.

Trillions of charged water particles rubbed past each other as the clouds became devastating electrical generators. When the energy became too much to bear, they released a one million volt bolt of lightning that travelled at two hundred thousand miles an hour directly toward Tom's boat.

In a fraction of a second, the lightning found the only metal object on the bay, hitting the top of the Oceanis's mast and exploded like a bomb.

Three hours later, Jan Lucas watched a Coast Guard Cutter moor onto their dock. She could do nothing but watch, shaking in terror, until the boat was tied off.

One of the officers climbed off with a boy in his arms. She ran toward him to find a rosy-cheeked Lucas.

'Momma!' he called to his crying mother.

She grabbed the boy up and squeezed him tight.

'He's okay, ma'am,' the Coast Guard officer told her. 'Just some scrapes and bruises. Our doctor has cleared him.'

'Where's my husband?' Jan asked in a small voice.

The officer looked down at his shoes for a moment, then met her eyes.

'We are still searching, ma'am. Did he wear a life jacket on the boat?'

Jan immediately knew the answer to that question. Tom liked to say, "Life jackets! Ha! I think I'll just stay in the boat, if that's okay."

She shook her head.

The officer held her gaze for a few more moments, nodded his head and looked away.

"Just stay on the boat." Jan recounted her husband's words again.

'We have to get back out there. I'll come back later tonight,' he told her.

Jan Harding didn't hear him. She already knew she'd be raising her son alone. Three days later, the search was abandoned, and the body of Thomas Hardy was never found. The report declared something about tidal flows and undercurrents, but it didn't really matter to Jan. Tom was gone and never coming back. Tidal flow or no tidal flow, nothing would change that fact.

From that day on, young Lucas developed a macabre fascination for all forms of natural energy. As the years passed, the fascination became an obsession.

He read everything he could find on electromagnet energy, particle physics, gravity, and later studied the work at the Hadron Collider into quantum fields.

Most boy's heroes were sports stars; for Lucas they were Einstein, Tesla, and particle physicists.

Jan was a practical woman and became very concerned for her son. She knew the world would eat him alive if all he knew were books. Lucas had also developed a deep shyness, avoiding people at all costs. To make matters worse, he frequently wet his bed y.

She knew she must act and drove him to the local karate school.

'Lucas's father is no longer with us,' Jan told Sensei Dan. 'He is withdrawn and depressed. Can you help him?'

Sensei Dan was a good man. He knew young men needed three things in life; discipline, strength, and confidence. Upon meeting young Lucas, Dan could see Lucas was in a world of pain.

Sensei Dan had his mission to save the boy. He had worked with many children who had lost their footing in this world and knew exactly what to do.

'Your mother tells me you're a bookworm and you piss the bed,' Dan told him. 'This will be fucked for you in high school when the bullies start eating your lunch. After that, you will become their plaything until they break you. Do you want to have some fun and stop that shit before it starts?'

No adult had ever spoken to Lucas like that, and he was very impressed. Dan had triggered a primal element in Lucas that was lost that afternoon in the storm.

The boy could only stare back at his musclebound karate master.

'Rule one; don't look directly into my eyes. Keep your eyes low unless you want the back of my hand,' Dan told him. 'Now show me how many push-ups you can do. Then you and I are going for a run. I hope you like pain because it's going to love you!'

For reasons Lucas didn't understand, he gave it up for Sensei Dan.

He worked his hardest to meet the challenges Sensei Dan set him. His young body endured many cycles of pain and growth until six months later Lucas morphed through several stages of transformation.

After a year, his anxiety, shyness, and bedwetting became distant memories. For that, Dan rewarded the boy through grading after grading until he reached his final goal. A black belt.

As the years passed, Lucas never needed his karate for self-defence.

Like sewer rats, school bullies had an innate sense for self-preservation. They viewed his body shape and swagger, instinctively knowing to keep clear of him. Lucas did, however, needed to rescue a few of his geeky friends from time to time.

But the bullies learned that lesson too and stayed away from the entire science gang.

It was then he met a girl named Tracey, and Tracey decided she was in love with him. Lucas was not very advanced in the romance stakes and didn't really have much say in the matter.

Tracey was not the most beautiful girl in school, and far from the coolest. Her parents owned the local store and lived in a trailer park.

Tracey was an energetic, freckled blonde. She was always keen on wrestling or other physical adventures. Her adventures included leading young Lucas down the path of sexual exploration.

Where Lucas was terrified of sex and very naive, Tracey was not.

Every time Tracey touched him, he got an erection that would endure for an eternity. Much of Lucas's time with Tracey was spent with a pillow, hat, or school bag covering his lap.

Even later in life, Lucas was never sure if Tracey wanted him to shift the pillows and bags. Nonetheless, Lucas was obsessed with her, and the pair were inseparable.

No matter what daily life events transpired, Lucas and Tracey always ended up together. Then one sunny day, Lucas knocked on Tracey's door and saw moving crates.

Having lost his father in a flash of light, he now lost Tracey to a big white moving truck and a loaded station wagon.

The pair wrote letters and made phone calls for months. Lucas learned from a young age what love was. As it turned out, love was obsession, a desperate sense of loss that caused physical nausea.

Love was a sadness too deep for tears to reach.

Jan Harding watched this process from a discreet distance. She knew her words were useless, so she simply offered comfort. In her experience, ice cream and weekend cable movie binges were the only antidote. She could only hope that time would take care of the rest. So, she gave him that time. Time without pressure to heal or irritating parental advice.

As the years passed, Lucas kept himself busy in the high school science club where he spent time with boys and girls like him. His group travelled across America winning science competitions.

In the small hours of the morning, when sleep abandoned him, Lucas was either thinking about Tracey, or he was back on the boat that fateful afternoon as the storm raged about him and his father.

On other nights, he would awake with a yell after being chased by malevolent streaks of blinding light, and the final, inevitable, explosion that blew him into the air.

Then one night, Lucas had a different dream.

He was studying zero-point energy; or vacuum energy, as it was known. Several presentations were made on the subject. One presentation demonstrated energy in the empty vacuum box. No matter was in the empty box, yet it was alive with boundless visible fields of energy.

Lucas's dream showed him converting the charged particle frequencies in the vacuum to sound. He lay in his deep slumber listening to the music of the universe.

Then his father appeared.

'Play the music, Lucas,' his father told him. 'Make the music yours.'

Lucas awoke with a start.

He lay panting, for several seconds as he recalled the dream and his father's words.

Make the music yours, played over and over in his head.

Everyone in the world of physics said vacuum energy cannot be harnessed. That the potential energy was held apart in fields of self-cancelling forces.

Now, Lucas knew it was because they were thinking like charged particle physicists. In his startling moment of clarity, Lucas saw the truth.

Energy is only the by-product. The true power is in the vibration. It is in the music.

At five a.m., he called his best friends and study partners John Carol and Kurt Hangle. The boys knew when Lucas called them at five a.m. not to argue, so they both dressed and met Lucas at the local bakery.

The baker was already well into his morning breadmaking and was happy when the sleepless boys came down to argue physics. He didn't understand any of it, but he loved the company.

When the boys arrived, Lucas was waiting for them with a sketch pad full of rough drawings and equations.

'You know that the best minds in particle physics have been working vacuum energy for over a hundred years,' Kurt told him.

'I know, right!' Lucas said enthusiastically, grinning like a mad man. 'But they were all looking in the wrong direction!'

Kurt and John simply stared back, waiting patiently.

'Accessing the energy fields is not about disrupting charged-energy balance using charged particles. It's about interacting with the energy fields using vibration,' Lucas announced, sitting back in his chair throwing his arms in the air. 'We are going to play the field's music!'

'Fuck this!' Kurt told him. 'I'm going back to bed.'

'No, wait,' John Carol told him. 'Einstein and Tesla both said, to understand the universe we must think in terms of energy and vibration. Lucas may be onto something.'

'We are going to build a resonance chamber and extract energy from the universe using an oscillating range of vibration resonance,' Lucas told them. 'But first we are going to need some serious math and a very big computer. Check out some of the equations I've started working on.'

John and Kurt read the numbers Lucas had created.

'Could this be right?' John asked numbly.

Kurt picked up the page and followed the equations with his finger. He looked up and smiled.

'We need to rock the shit out of this thing!' Kurt told them.

The Interview

'Unless my memory fails me, wasn't it the German physicist Max Planck who introduced the concept of zero-point energy way back in 1911. Since then, physicists all over the world have claimed it's inaccessible as a power source. How an earth did you make it work?' Rowland Smith asked.

'Firstly, let's give credit where credit is due. It all started with Nikola Tesla and his most famous quote; "To understand the universe you must think in terms of energy, frequency and vibration," Lucas replied.

'I read that Tesla was born in a thunderstorm,' Smith added. 'That he had a rare memory skill, allowing him to design inventions in his head without the need for testing them.'

'That's true,' Lucas affirmed. 'In fact, he was right ninety percent of the time. He was born in a thunderstorm, and he inherited that rare memory capacity from his mother.'

'So, how did you access the elusive vacuum energy?' Smith asked.

'We played it music,' Lucas said with simple smile. 'We used frequency vibration across a spectrum that resonated with the particles until the balance in the energy-field barrier was collapsed.'

'Incredible!' Smith said. 'Was your discovery made in the labs of CalTech?

'Ah, CalTech,' Lucas mused. 'That was where we first built and tested our early algorithms. It was also when we met the US government for the first time.'

'I think we all want to hear this story,' Smith said enthusiastically.

California Institute of Technology (CalTech), Pasadena.

Lucas, John, and Kurt were gathered around a computer discussing test data as it emerged on screen, when the lab door burst open and two men in black suits marched in.

'Lucas Harding?' one of the men called.

Lucas looked up from his screen and viewed the man.

'Yes?' he answered firmly.

'I'm Federal Agent Thomas. We need to speak with you. Come with us please.'

'What the hell's going on?' Lucas was perplexed by this intrusion. 'How did you get in here?'

'Come with us now or I will arrest you,' the agent told him.

Lucas Harding stood and looked to his friends. They were stunned and nervous. Lucas locked eyes with John Carol, his project partner and best friend. Carol could only shrug.

The agents led Lucas to an interview room off the main Caltech administration building. Waiting in the room were two other men, also in dark suits.

'That'll be all,' said a distinguished looking middle-aged man.

The arresting agents left the room and closed the door. Lucas suddenly felt trapped.

'Have a seat, Mr Harding,' the older agent told him.

Lucas fumbled with a chair that half tipped over. He recovered the chair and sat.

'My name is Terrance Wolf. I work for the federal government and if our little chat goes well, this will be the last time you see me.'

Lucas was developing a deep nausea in his stomach. He sensed that he and his team were in danger.

'I... I'm not sure what this is about,' Lucas began, 'but you have no right...'

Wolf ignored him.

'We have been following your progress, Mr Harding,' Wolf told him. 'Congratulations, it seems you have broken the code to unlocking zero-point energy.'

Lucas knew by the tone in Wolf's voice that he was not actually being congratulated for anything.

'Did you know that dozens of physicists, just like yourself, have been down the path you are now on?' Wolf asked.

Lucas's brain began to reel. What is Wolf saying?

'Have you wondered why all the contemporary data published on accessing zero-point energy is negative? Why no physicist on the planet is working on breaking down the zero-point energy barrier?' Wolf asked him.

Lucas Harding stared back at Wolf perplexed.

He knew the internet was alive with academics discussing the theories of accessing quantum energy, but it was true, no one had ever fully developed a working prototype. In fact, he'd noticed over the years that many videos on this work had mysteriously vanished from the web.

None the less, Lucas did not have time for Terrance Wolf. He had work to do and this current debate was not getting him any closer to his goals.

'Please state your business here, or I'll call security,' Lucas demanded. 'Our work here is privately funded by the university, and the government has no business here.'

'You're a once in a generation thinker, Mr Harding. Therefore, I won't need to wax this.

'You and your team are in breach of national security.'

'What?' Lucas almost yelled.

'I'm sorry. Can't you hear me?'

'We are theoretical scientists working on an algorithm that could change how the world generates electricity. How can that possibly be in breach of anything!'

Wolf stared back at him with flat eyes.

'Please tell me you're not wasting my time,' Lucas told him, beginning to regain some confidence.

'Mr Harding, listen to me carefully.' Wolf's voice was deadpan, almost robotic. 'Your government does not want you to continue research on vibration resonance and vacuum energy. The fact you have been allowed to develop the concept thus far amazes me.'

Lucas was beginning to feel genuine anger. This was not an emotion he experienced very often.

Wolf continued in his deadpan voice.

'The entire economic structure of this world is based on the burning of consumable fossil fuels to light and heat homes, make machines function, and drive industry. Therefore you, Mr Harding, will not be creating a free-energy solution.'

Lucas Harding felt blood rush to his head.

'Are you crazy?' Lucas yelled. 'We have passed the global warming tipping point! Are you telling me that my government wants to keep burning fossil fuels, even if a universal clean solution might be available?'

'Mr Harding, shut the fuck up!' Wolf yelled at him.

Harding was rocked back in his chair by the sheer violence in Wolf's voice. Wolf adjusted his tie and nodded to a second, unidentified man. Lucas went rigid.

The second man handed Wolf a thick dossier. Wolf opened it with great deliberation and began reading its contents.

'June 1995,' Wolf began. 'Doctor Theodore A. Pershing was to present this paper to the world. He died in a single car accident that very day. This document is what remains of his work.'

Wolf lay the file on the desk. At once, Lucas recognized the algorithm. It was almost identical to his own.

'October 1999, Doctor Jackson Hall attempted to present this paper. He was found dead in his bathtub of an apparent heart attack just a few hours before he left the house. His family claimed he was in perfect health.'

Wolf laid out a second document. Again, Lucas recognized the equation.

'Do I need to continue?' Wolf asked.

Lucas could see there were at least a dozen more documents in the folder. He looked back at Wolf and slumped in his chair. His mouth was dry, and he wanted to be sick.

'Get him a glass of water,' Wolf told one of his men. Wolf waited in silence until the water arrived.

'Have some water, Mr Harding,' Wolf advised. 'Now, for the upside.'

Lucas Harding half raised his eyes.

'Have you heard about the new CIA Labs?' Wolf asked the defeated young man.

'Of course,' Lucas told him in a small voice.

'The United States is currently facing a tech war. A war we are not currently winning. To attract young minds, minds like yours, CIA Labs is offering some very attractive research grants. These packages are only available to the very best people in their respective fields.'

Like water poured onto stone, Wolf's words did not penetrate Lucas Harding's shocked mind. He was terrified and appalled in equal doses. Could this be happening? Was he dreaming?

'We need to build superconductors and wireless energy fields for a new generation of supercomputers,' Wolf continued. 'You will have an unlimited budget and the freedom to recruit your own team. Those who can clear a top-secret clearance review, of course.'

Lucas sat back in his chair attempting to digest the offer and weigh his options. 'Would you like some coffee?' Wolf asked. 'Black, one sugar. Is that right?' Lucas stared at the agent with contempt, as Wolf demonstrated his full dominance.

'You want me to build levitating magnet conductors and Wi-Fi energy fields?' Lucas asked. 'For what purpose? Railguns on warships?'

'We already have that shit,' Wolf replied dismissively. 'Your work will be used for cyber defence purposes only. Not weapons. We need AI supercomputers to outthink the new hacking programmes the Chinese have planned for us.'

Wolf gave Lucas a moment to think.

'We need a whole new generation of high-speed, intuitive AI thinking machines,' Wolf continued. 'Computers that don't run off conventional programming, but ones that create solutions in nanoseconds.'

The coffee arrived, and Wolf took out a packet of cigarettes.

'You can't smoke in here,' Lucas told him.

Wolf chuckled and lit up. Lucas watched the cloud of blue smoke fill the small room, making him cough. He muttered something obscene, then drank his coffee in silence.

'China has over one million genius-level scientists in their population,' Wolf announced. 'We can't be sure how many are working in weaponized tech, but needless to say, the US is outnumbered.'

Wolf threw his cigarette on the floor and ground it out with his shoe. He stood up and adjusted his belt.

'The next war won't be fought with guns and missiles, Mr Harding. It will be fought in cyber space. Almost every day, foreign hackers shut down elements of our business or government structures. If we are to survive, we need young men like you working for us.'

Lucas considered himself a patriotic American and was more than happy to do his part. But knew his clean energy project was far more important than a tit-for-tat cyber war with China.

'I still don't get it,' he told Wolf. 'My team is working on harnessing the energy of the universe on a macro scale to save global warming. You know, to save the whole planet, so that your grandchildren with have somewhere to live!'

Wolf smiled and nodded.

'So that you understand. This is the policy of the US government. Policy that was formed well above my paygrade. I am simply a tool in this, and there's no point trying to negotiate with me.'

Lucas Harding knew he was defeated. The vault door was slammed shut and he was officially taken off the field.

'The work I'm offering you will be challenging enough and most importantly,' Wolf's voice took on a sharp edge once again, 'if you do it for me, and don't try to fuck me in any way, you won't end up like these poor saps.'

Wolf tapped the documents on the desk, locking eyes with Lucas.

'Even if I don't kill you,' Wolf continued, 'try to imagine spending twenty-three hours a day in a nine by six feet box with no internet or reading materials. Very few people we have in these cells last a year without going completely insane.'

Wolf sat down and crossed his legs. He saw that Lucas understood his position.

'You will be sent employment contracts over the next few days. In the meantime, keep your mouth shut about everything we have spoken about,' Wolf warned him. 'Cheer up, Mr Harding! The pay is great. In no time, you and your pals will become quite rich men.'

Lucas Harding was released from the interrogation and took the long, lonely walk back to his lab. The agents were gone, and his team was waiting for him.

'Oh my God! What the hell was that?' John Carol asked.

John could see that Lucas was ghost white and very nervous. Lucas looked at him blankly.

'Not here. We must go outside.'

The team walked the corridors in silence, until they reached an outdoor lunch park. They sensed a major event had occurred but remained quiet.

Reaching a park area, everyone sat on the two facing benches. Lucas's head was down. He felt sick.

'I just met some very dark people who I guessed, were CIA agents,' he said in a small voice.

'The CIA?' John was perplexed. 'What the hell does the CIA want here?'

'They gave me a very strong message. We are to stop work on our research,' Lucas told him. 'If I say any more, I will be endangering your lives.'

'What the fuck are you talking about, Luc? Are you mad?' Kurt asked. John Carol stood up and began to pace.

'Is this what I think it is?' John asked. 'Did we get too close? Are we threatening their precious petrochemical industry'.

Lucas did not respond. His head was lowered, looking at the ground. As his friends raged, he watched two ants tugging on an old crust of bread from different directions. The ants were the same size and weight. As a result, the bread went nowhere.

'What the hell did they say to you, Lucas?' Kurt asked. 'You look like you've seen a ghost.'

Lucas looked up at his friends with defeat in his eyes. For most of their young lives, Lucas had been their rock. He steadfastly held his ground against all their critics and naysayers.

"They threatened you, didn't they?' Kurt asked grimly.

'They threatened all of us. And I mean all the way threatened us.'

The Interview

Rowland Smith shook his head in disbelief.

'My head is reeling! I have so many questions. Firstly, how on earth did you find the courage to continue? How are you able to talk about this now?'

Lucas smiled and nodded.

'We were young and so very close to our goals.'

'Yes, but how did you escape the clutches of these government agents?' Smith asked.

'Divine intervention,' Lucas told him sincerely.

'In what form did this intervention take?' Smith played along.

'It took the form of one Mackenzie James.' Lucas smiled to himself. 'Or, Mack, as he insisted on being called.'

'We knew Mackenzie James,' Smith told him. 'The green energy magnate. I interviewed him several times and he was a friend of our show.'

'He was an improbable character,' Lucas told Smith. 'Did you know he was voted least likely to succeed in his early high school years? Then Mack hit the books and became a fighter pilot after 9/11. He was one of dozens of navy pilots who saw UAPs flying without any means of conventional propulsion.'

'I ran a report about them years ago,' Smith confirmed. 'All those navy pilot reports, and the Pentagon videos. The government reports claimed they don't know what they are.'

'The UAPs were the driving force behind Mack's quest for light-energy,' Lucas said.

'I think its's time we learned more about Mackenzie James,' Smith suggested.

From the commencement of the Iraq war, Mack's carrier battle group was assigned to interdict enemy operations and provide ground support.

His precision bombs saved countless American lives in the nonstop round robin of launch, bomb, land, and rearm.

After one devastating mission, Mack was back onboard his carrier taking a long, hot shower. He was nearing the end of his rotation and exhausted in every possible way.

While he shaved, Mack caught his reflection in the polished steel mirror. A much older man stared back at him.

'You're not a boy anymore,' his flight commander, Jake Townsend commented as he entered the room.

'I haven't been a boy for a while now,' Mack told him without a hint of emotion. 'You know I blew up a village yesterday. I saw it on CNN. A whole fucking village full of people because a marine squad took some sniper fire.'

'So what? That's your job. We provide air support to the guys on the ground,' Jake told him.

'My job is to kill our enemy, not blow-up villages full of civilians,' Mack replied with an icy edge in his voice. 'A two thousand pound bomb straight down the middle from thirty thousand feet. They didn't stand a chance.'

Mack splashed cold water on his face.

'You know, they haven't found a single WMD facility. Or any evidence there was any to begin with' Mack's tone was dead. 'This whole war is looking like a giant White House lie.'

Jake Townsend was an experienced combat leader. He knew all the signs of a man approaching the end of his tether. Mack had just mouthed off to him and accused the President of the United States of being a liar.

This behaviour might work in the boardroom of a Wall Street investment firm, but out here, in the middle of a war, talk like this leads to disaster for a man in charge of a forty-ton fighter plane.

'We've been bombing enemy positions for months now. How are you sleeping?' Jake asked.

'Sleep!' Mack laughed out loud for far too long. He laughed until tears rolled down his cheeks.

Jake shook his head.

'Okay, that's enough! You're on the beach,' Jake told the younger man. 'Pack your shit. You're on leave, as of right now.'

Mack stared at his reflection in the mirror. He wanted to protest, to stay with his team, and do his duty. But he couldn't speak. All he could see was the massive cloud of dust he left behind in the Iraqi desert.

Jake patted Mack gently on the shoulder and walked out. He knew that after a few cocktails and a week of sunbaking in Hawaii Mack would be sorted out. He would return to the squadron full of his usual piss and vinegar.

Jake Townsend was wrong. Lieutenant Mackenzie James would never fly in combat again. That afternoon, Mack launched off the flight deck in a Grumman C-2 Greyhound and an hour later landed in Riyadh Air Base, Saudi Arabia. The next day he caught a lift on a C-17A Globemaster to Pearl Harbour, Hawaii.

'How was your flight, sir?' A young gangly, red-haired airman asked him upon landing.

'Long, loud, and fucked up in every possible way,' Mack told him.

'Excellent! Welcome to Pearl!' The airman was having fun. 'We thank you for choosing to fly US Airlift Command. While in Pearl we recommend AVIS car hire and a visit to our war museum.'

'Yeah, yeah. The old jokes are the best,' Mack told the young man.

'That they are, sir! There's a shuttle to your billet in front of the main building. Have a great day!'

Mack looked up at the young man and couldn't help but smile. It was nice being back in a world where people had time for jokes. He wondered if his sense of humour would ever return.

After two days of batting the breeze and drinking cocktails with other leave pilots, Mack started getting restless.

The next morning, he woke with a cloudy hangover and decided he needed to sweat. He headed to the gym where he punished his body for an hour. The moist subtropical heat made him sweat a river. He could literally feel the evil of combat leaving his body.

Exhausted and feeling cleansed, he took himself for a swim in the cool sea. As the water hit him, he knew he was ready to go back to work.

He dressed in a fresh uniform and made his way to the main administration building.

'What are my options, ma'am?' Mack asked the base personnel officer.

'You have five years in, out of the mandatory six,' Captain Jen Hadden told him. 'Your proficiency scores are high, and your record is clean. This means you can apply to become a flight instructor. But that process will take a year. Or you can go into the general flight rotation here at Pearl or Japan.'

Japan. That sounds interesting, Mack mused. He always wanted to visit Tokyo. A week later, Mack was being checked out in an older F-18 at Naval Air Facility, Atsugi, Japan. His assignment was not glamorous, mostly flight-testing refitted engines and ferrying aircraft to the awaiting carriers.

The relaxed workload gave him time to recuperate and to think. Mother Nature, however, had other ideas.

At 2.49 p.m. on 11 March, 2011, an undersea rupture of tectonic plates along the Japan Trench measuring approximately one hundred and ninety miles long by ninety-five miles wide lurched upward some one hundred and sixty-four feet.

The event displaced a huge bolt of water that morphed into a series of tsunami waves that began their unstoppable march toward the Japanese coast, and the rest became history.

Mack had just landed an F-18 on his carrier that was inside the tsunami circle. The ocean was deep there and the ship passed over the waves without difficulty.

Mack was making his way to the mess for a well-earned cup of coffee when a fellow pilot rushed out to greet him.

'Dude! You've got to see this!'

Mack followed his shipmate to the mess to watch live as the disaster unfolded on shore. He watched the water destroy the towns and people; it then reached the nuclear power stations.

The fighter pilots on the carriers were powerless to help. They had to stand by impotently and watch the ships' rescue helicopters race toward shore to rescue the stranded people.

For several days after the quake, the US navy helicopters delivered food and water and lifted survivors to safety.

Mack, once again, had time on his hands. He worked out hard every day. He read everything in the library, yet no matter what he did to keep himself busy, the memory of the UFO he and his flight saw that day in training flashed before his eyes.

One question kept playing though his mind on a continuous loop.

What powered these machines?

Then, like a bolt of lightning, he knew what he must do. He must find the energy force that fuelled the unknown craft that haunted his dreams.

Mack committed himself to his quest. But first he was going to need money. A lot of money.

Who has all the money? Mack asked himself over a cup of lousy navy coffee.

'Wall Street!' he said out loud. 'All the money is in Wall Street.'

Two or three other pilots looked at him with little interest. Everyone had been confined for too long and they were starting to lose it. Talking to yourself on board the carrier had become the new normal.

On one bright sunny day at sea, Mackenzie James's navy enlistment term expired.

His shipmates threw him a party in a shady Tokyo nightclub. They hired him a stripper named; well, Mack had forgotten her name, and he woke up a civilian.

The next day he got to work creating his dream of building a green energy empire.

He took an internship with a large investment banking and capital venture firm where he learned the machinations of making money.

Vast sums of money.

For fifteen long years, he divided his time between the study of clean energy engineering and the raising of venture capital for such projects.

Using all his wit and charm, Mack extracted millions of dollars from the wealthiest New York and global investors.

He flew to several countries where green energy projects were being built. He witnessed Big Energy lobbyists brow beat politicians, employing every dirty trick in the book to keep oil, gas, and coal front and centre.

Despite this, Mack saw that the people wanted green energy. They wanted hydro, wind, and solar. They knew climate change was real, as the storms and floods wrecked their homes.

In the meantime, Mack built his own portfolio, until the day came when he became wealthier than many of his clients.

It was then he met Angelina Cohen on a solar farm fact finding mission to Israel. The Israelis were using the desert sun to generate electrical power using superheated fluids thermodynamically. They ran this fluid through bearing-less superconducting turbines. The power storage units they built were a new generation of hydrogen cells.

Just one of these solar farms could supply electricity to a city of fifty thousand homes.

The Israeli government placed a premium on internal security and assigned agents to mix with the foreign businessmen and women. Each agent was given an official role title so as to blend in.

Angelina Cohen acted as an Israeli assistant press officer. This gave her access to engage with the foreigners.

As the fact-finding tour wound down, the Israelis hosted a farewell cocktail party.

Mack had seen Ange several times during the tour. He had even exchanged a few words with her.

During the party, he watched her moving through the crowd. She spoke with this person and that. Touched the odd arm as she made a conversation point and laughed at their jokes.

Her male audience was captivated.

Ange wore a bright white, thigh-length silk dress that highlighted the curve of her body. The white dress provided a stunning contrast to her jet-black hair. Mack could see her legs were long and shapely, and her straight back drew up to wide shoulders that carried toned, olive tan arms.

Mack noticed his breathing had changed as he viewed her long, graceful body breezing around the room with an almost ethereal lightness.

He attempted to guess her height. She was taller than most of the other women and wore flat shoes. Mack knew this was common for tall girls, as she would easily be six foot in heels.

In a moment of clarity, Mack realized he had been staring at her for far too long. Too late, in a flash, her eyes were on him.

Angelina Cohen held her gaze on him for perhaps one second longer than was strictly necessary, causing Mack to stop breathing.

Mack recovered from his shock and fumbled with his facial muscles. He managed to form something resembling a smile in return.

In the time it took him to get his face organized, Angelina had already moved on, continuing her circuit, and ignoring him once again.

Mack was now fully distracted. He attempted to show interest in his quorum but kept flashing glances toward Angelina. Was that real? Did she look at him that way?

'Grow up, man! You're here for business,' he muttered to himself.

Mack excused himself and went to the bar for a real drink. He ordered a Johnny Walker Blue, straight up, no ice. Only a barbarian would water down a shot of Blue.

The barman nodded in salute and reached high on the shelf.

As Mack watched the silky amber flow into his glass, he considered which energy project partner he would focus on next. Raising capital was a retail exercise. It was as much about personal relationships, as it was about investment dollars and profit forecasts.

Get the wrong partner and the deal would become buried in… He suddenly became aware of a warm presence beside him.

'Hey! What's up?' Angelina Cohen asked him brightly, like a girl at a beach bar. Mack sipped his scotch wrong, and spluttered. He coughed twice and attempted a recovery. It didn't work, and he had to wipe his chin.

'Well, that was cool…' Mack muttered to himself, feeling like a goofy teenager. Angelina giggled gently.

'You have a little…' She indicated by touching her chin.

Mack wiped it, then had no idea what to do with his hand, so he wiped it on the bar mat.

'Can we do that again? I'm Mack, and you are?'

'Ange. I'm with the Israeli press office. We spoke a few times but haven't been introduced.'

'I remember. Can I buy you a drink?'

'Strictly forbidden.' She frowned and shook her head. 'Then again, we must all live a little dangerously now and then. Don't you agree?'

Mack smiled. He liked small talk code; dangerously is a word only used when dangerous behaviour is contemplated.

'I really do,' Mack told her. 'What's your poison?'

'Fast cars and confident men,' she told him. 'But tonight, I'll settle for a whiskey.'

Her voice was rich and smooth, much like the aged whisky she ordered. Her accent carried a mix of exotic Middle Eastern tones yet was highly Americanized.

The pair silently watched the barman pour a second glass.

'I watched you working the room,' Mack told her. She smirked, keeping her eyes on the drink.

'I know,' she said quietly. 'I saw you watching me.'

'You have a way with people. They were captivated by you,' he continued.

'People are easy, if you know how to stroke them,' she purred. Then turned to face him.

Mack indulged himself by absorbing her face. A range of emotions began pulling at him from multiple directions. A romantic may have said he was hit by lightning. Yet, Mack did not consider himself romantic. He was a stone-cold businessman.

Then why is my heart racing? he asked himself.

To say Mack and Ange chatted for hours would not have been completely accurate.

The truth was, the great Mackenzie James was reduced to nothing more than an eager puppy in the presence of Angelina Cohen. He chased every stick she threw him, and Ange was very good at throwing sticks.

Everything she offered had either a hint of possibilities, or clues to Mack's next question. Her conversational style swung between refined lady and streetwise tramp, with little segue slides between the two.

Mack was kept busy, trying to guess which persona to aim for. To elevate the challenge, Ange deliberately oscillated between them unpredictably and often.

All the while, Mack was putting her together; doubting she was an assistant press officer. Ange didn't act like an assistant to anyone. He also guessed she'd spent time with the boys, and they did not make her nervous.

She knew exactly what to say and how to say it. But there was something else he saw in her; she never said anything she didn't intend to. Ange was always in complete control of her words and responses.

Adding to the mix; there was something tough about this girl. She was physical and competitive, yet she was hiding something. Her polished and practiced behaviour indicated she had built a wall.

This wall, Mack presumed, protected her from the world.

Other people joined their group, vying for Mack's attention. But they all ended up chatting with Ange. Yet, Ange always maintained close physical contact with him. Even with her back to him, Mack could smell her scent of green apples and cinnamon.

This spicy tang danced up and down his cerebral cortex like a low frequency hum. He was becoming exhausted by the intensity of emotions she evoked in him.

Standing with her back to him, she dropped her arm until her fingers touched his hand. Mack shuddered at the touch. He straightened his back and took a deep breath. Ange flicked her head around and flashed him the briefest of smiles, before returning to her conversation.

Mack took a long pull on his whisky. With one simple touch of her hand, he was hooked.

Eventually, the party began to break up. Mack's associates knew to take their leave, and by eleven p.m., Mack and Ange were alone. He knew if this, whatever this was, went to the next level, Ange would be in charge. So, he played the gentleman and let her run with it.

'Well, it's getting late,' he stretched and yawned, throwing down the gauntlet.

'Yeah, I'm off too.' But she didn't move. She just looked into his face with her large amber eyes and smiled with her perfect mouth.

On that night, Mack experienced a rare moment of humility. He knew the gods had colluded and granted him an extraordinary gift. In their typically random and unpredictable fashion, they placed him in the presence of Angelina Cohen, and let biology do the rest.

By midnight, Mack and Ange were locked together in a physical and emotional universe. No earthly thing existed for them for a very long time.

The Interview

'She became was Mack's lover and aide-de-camp,' said Lucas.

'An enigmatic lady to be sure,' replied Smith. 'What's her story?'

'Her story is more a saga! She was with us from the start, playing a critical role in the project, and a whole lot more.'

Isla Mocha — Off the Chilean Coast

The one hundred and sixty mile round trip from Temuco to Isla Mocha was a comfortable ride aboard Mackenzie James's Bell 429 Helicopter.

Mack wanted to lease ten acres of land on Mocha. The offer Mack made the Chilean government was generous and straight forward. Mack knew who to bribe, who to flatter, and who to reassure that the project was far from nefarious.

On board the flight was the Chilean Ministry of the Interior official, a mid-ranking admiral of the navy, and a director of Banco Estella. They all had a sizable personal stake in making this deal work. After all, if a crazy American wanted to pay exorbitant prices for small piece of a useless island, who really cares?

The island appeared beyond the chopper's windscreen. The interior hills maintained some residual morning mist, giving the island a primordial aura. If a herd of tyrannosaurs ran out on the plains, nobody would have been surprised.

Mack performed a slow orbit of the island before heading inland. The party viewed the beautiful coastal flats and beaches, then the high peaks to the valley area in the centre and their landing site.

They saw cabins and local farmers going about their morning chores. Some of the people looked up but were not impressed by this noisy machine interrupting their peace and quiet.

As they crossed the peak of the mountains, Mack checked his Navman. He adjusted his course as he descended toward his final waypoint.

The proposed building site was mildly undulating, but he knew the heavy bulldozers would make short work of that.

Below them, three men in yellow hardhats were reading a site plan but gave up as the prop blast hit them. One man folded the map and put it away. It was Jeff Tyndall, his project manager.

Mack flew competently toward the helipad, balancing the flight controls with ease, and with a couple of bumps placed the skids near enough to the centre.

Tyndall was close now, waiting for Mack to kill the power. He was a capable looking guy, burly and square jawed.

As they disembarked the chopper, Mack introduced everyone.

'Okay, Jeff,' Mack declared. 'This is your show, you can play tour guide.'

'Sure, Mack. My pleasure. Welcome everyone,' Tyndall told them.

Tyndall guided the visitors to an outdoor table and spread out a construction plan. He spent the next twenty minutes translating the map as to where everything was going on the ground. The Chileans were satisfied with what they saw. It all conformed with the agreement they had made with Mack.

'Once the ground has been prepared,' Tyndall told them. 'The buildings will arrive prefabricated. The modules will arrive by sea and unloaded over a period of two days using the CH-53 Sea Stallion your navy has generously leased us.'

Tyndall nodded toward the admiral, who gave a curt nod in the return. He was pleased to help, after all the commission he charged paid for a brand new fifty-foot fishing boat.

'Well gentleman, that looks like lunch!' Mack told them.

Mack and Ange went back to the chopper and returned with picnic baskets. They ate fresh seafood, antipasti, and crusty bread coated in olive oil. The food was washed down with a spicy local red wine. All except Mack, of course, who had to fly them home.

'To be clear,' the admiral began. 'This site is not to be used for the making of anything illegal. We can support and protect you, but no illegal activities.'

'This is a pure science research site, Admiral,' Mack told him firmly. 'We are here to test clean energy theories only. Nothing illegal will occur here, and you are free to inspect us at any time.'

The admiral took another look around and nodded. It was getting cold, and he had a dinner engagement to attend back in Santiago that night.

The interior official still looked sceptical.

'It is still a little strange why you can't do this on American soil,' he commented.

'There are very powerful people in my country who do not want this research performed,' Mack told him. 'I promise you this; we will be sharing our results with your government. If we are successful, you stand to make a lot of money here.'

Money was money, the minister agreed. Who was he to complain?

The Interview

'To recap; you were offered a contract with CIA Labs, building advanced technology to combat cyber threats,' Rowland Smith began.

'Unlimited funding, pure research, and my own team,' Lucas confirmed. 'Not a bad offer in the scheme of things.'

'So, what happened?' Smith asked.

'Mackenzie James entered my world,' Lucas said simply.

'Ah, I see,' Smith said with a grin.

'Well not actually Mack at first, but his partner in crime, Angelina Cohen.'

'That sounds like fun?' Smith offered.

'Fun may not be right word,' said Lucas.

To build the CIA labs, the agency tapped into the cyber technology hub of America, establishing operations in Palo Alto, California.

Every other day Lucas Harding cycled to the ByteMe gym to de-stress and clear his mind. Unlike many of his friends, he liked the blinged-up style of the place. There were plenty of nerdy guys building muscles and hot tech girls.

It was a Thursday when Lucas finished his final pull-down rep set and was about to start stretching. He went into a lunge when a tall redhead walked past.

Lucas lost his stretch count.

As she went by, her phone dropped onto the carpet. But she kept walking.

Lucas swooped down and grabbed it, moving after the girl. He called to her but noticed she had ear buds in, so he touched her arm.

She spun around and met the young man's eyes. Lucas felt his heart stop.

'You, ah, you dropped your phone,' he managed to tell her. The girl looked down at his hand holding the phone.

'You just dropped it,' he said.

The name Angelina Cohen was on many intelligence community databases, so when she travelled, Ange used an alias. Today, Ange was Debbie Levin, an Israeli student looking for a summer internship in Silicon Valley.

'Lucas, listen to me,' Ange/Debbie said. 'Put the phone in your pocket and I'll call you in thirty minutes. Don't be in your office, or your apartment.'

'What? How did you know my name? This is your phone. You dropped it, and I just picked it up.'

'Lucas, shut up and listen to me,' she told the young man. 'A very important person wants to talk about vacuum energy and vibration resonance, do you understand? Take the call outside and away from other people.'

Ange turned on her heels and left Lucas standing with his mouth gapping open.

In the following minutes, Lucas played the conversation over in his head, and began conjuring up outcomes.

Was this a CIA trap? Were they setting him up? Some kind of loyalty test? What's the downside of taking the call? What if the girl is a spy? If he takes the call, will he be implicated?

This deal was beginning to suck. But his scientific curiosity was eating at him. *What if this was real?*

Lucas wanted a shower, but realized he couldn't leave the phone unattended. Not even in his locker. The thing was potentially dynamite, so he dressed over his sweaty body, got on his bike, and rode to a nearby park.

Minutes later the phone rang. He pressed the answer key.

'Lucas?' Ange asked.

'Yes.'

'My name is Angelina. This phone is secure and no one else is listening. I work for a man who is very interested in your work. He knows about your progress and that your government has shut you down. Are you getting this?'

Lucas was shocked. He kept analysing the risk of continuing the conversation. Then thought, *keep going, you haven't done anything wrong yet.*

'Yes, I understand.'

'Good. I have a very important question for you. Do you want to meet this man and talk about continuing your research?' Her voice was quiet and measured.

Lucas knew this was the rub. He could be talking to the CIA, or a foreign agent. Either way, what he said next could result in prison for life or worse.

'Do you want your phone back?' he asked. 'Or shall I just hand it back to the CIA guys?'

'If you're as smart as Mackenzie James says you are,' Ange began, 'you'll listen to what I'm saying.'

Mackenzie James! Lucas knew the name instantly. Still, it meant nothing. This could still be a trap. He also realized he'd been talking for far too long. 'Angelina, or whatever your name is, this conversation is over.'

Lucas hung up and tossed the phone in a nearby trash can, then nervously made his way back to his lab.

It was a long trip. Every car and every person he saw may have been a CIA kill team.

All the same, a strange excitement set into his bones. That girl, the call, and the name Mackenzie James, all flashed around in his brain like a swirling storm. He wanted to do a Google search on him but realized it would leave a trail.

With no other course of action available to him, he spent all afternoon nervously waiting for a CIA security team to burst into his office and grab him.

At seven p.m., he left the lab and rode his bike three miles to his apartment. There again, he waited for the CIA.

He tried to eat but couldn't taste the food. He drank a beer and that seemed to help. So, he drank another.

Ten p.m. Still no CIA.

After a fitful night's sleep, he woke and took a shower. The heat of the water restored some of his calm, until the shower door swung open, seemingly of its own accord. It was Angelina Cohen!

'What the fuck!' he yelled.

His voice was pitched way too high, and he instantly felt a range of unmanly emotions as he stood stark naked before this imposing woman.

He covered his groin.

'Leave the water running and listen to me,' she told him. Lucas moved out of the shower stream as though in a dream. 'Get the fuck out of here! I told you; I'm not speaking to you!' Ange handed him a towel.

'My real name is Ange. I work for Mackenzie James, and this is not a trick or a test. He wants you to help him build and run a testing lab on an island in South America. I can't say where just yet.'

Lucas felt like he'd been slapped. The words testing lab in South America kept repeating in his brain.

'We know the position you are in and the dangers.' Ange was still speaking. This was not a dream. 'But we are talking about the future of the planet. Please, at least talk to Mack. If you are still concerned, you can walk away, and we'll never contact you again.'

Lucas stood in front of Ange feeling like a child. Even with a towel around his waist, he felt as naked as the day he was born.

'The phone I gave you yesterday is on your bed,' she told him. 'It is only connected to one number over an encoded satellite link. The password is "Frequency". When you are ready, go to an open area like yesterday, unlock the phone and press the green key. Mack will pick up.

Ange smiled at the bewildered scientist.

'Nice body by the way,' she told him and ruffled his hair.

It was then his towel fell from his waist, and Lucas was naked again. Ange giggled once, spun on her heels, and left.

'What in God's name is happening!' Lucas whispered to himself.

The Interview

'Quite a start to the day!' said Rowland Smith.

'Not my best moment! But you can say this about Ange; she knows how to get a guy's attention,' replied Lucas.

'So, you met with Mackenzie James? Ballsy move, deep diving into a CIA pond to drag you out.'

'He would have liked that; being called ballsy,' replied Lucas 'But he'd never admit it, of course.'

Lucas laughed at the thought.

'Okay, I get it. Don't leave us in suspense, get on with the story!'

Lucas continued. 'When I called Mack, he told me he was in the apartment next to mine. That he'd hacked the security cameras and CIA bugs. He told me to have a very normal day. To do exactly what I do every day and to simply walk into his apartment at nine that night.'

'Very clever,' said Smith 'I love the trade craft. He knew the CIA tracked you on the street. That your lab was being monitored, and your apartment was under surveillance. The safest place to hide was right next door! So, that's where you learned about the island?'

'Yes. I did what he said and had a very normal day. Then entered the apartment right on nine p.m.'

'You made it,' Mack said quietly and simply, giving Lucas his trademark smile.

To Lucas, Mack was already a legend. A self-made billionaire, all on the back of green energy. There were very few billionaires in this world who made their money elevating the human condition, and Mackenzie James was one of them.

At once, Lucas had a strange sensation. Since losing his father to a storm, Lucas had struggled to find a father figure. His karate sensei had transformed him from a frightened child and into a strong, confident teenager. But that was limit of their relationship.

Lucas had lecturers he had bonded with. There were uncles and older cousins who he liked, but no one had truly replaced his father.

The moment he saw Mack's face, he felt a special connection. It was as though he had been lost in the wilderness and finally made it home. Mackenzie James had come along just in time.

Over the period of one hour, Mack chatted about Lucas's work and outlined the escape plan.

In one seamless action, Lucas and his team were going to elude the CIA surveillance, make their escape from the American territories, and fly to a secluded island. The lab on the island was almost built and he, with his team, were going to set it up then build a free energy machine. His dream of a lifetime was now in sight.

'It's vital that you and your colleagues don't change your daily routines,' Mack insisted.

Ange was in the small kitchen of the apartment. She crossed into the living room carrying a sandwich she had made in a brown paper bag. She handed it to Lucas.

'Don't forget to eat it,' she told him. 'You need your strength.'

'Oh, thank you,' he told her and looked at her face. All he saw was warmth and concern looking back at him.

'You have a big job ahead of you.' Mack was speaking again, causing Lucas to refocus. 'You need to recruit only the scientists who are dedicated to this programme. They must be capable of living away from home for a very long time. Once you're gone, you can't contact anyone in America until the project is complete.'

Lucas considered this and nodded.

'When you talk to your colleagues, you need to be somewhere the CIA can't bug or track you electronically,' Ange told him.

'I have just the thing. We have a special code for private chats. We've been using it for months,' Lucas told them.

'Remember, the CIA have been conducting surveillance for a very long time,'

Ange warned him, 'Never underestimate them. The simple rule to remember is to leave no cracks. They are like water, and water always finds the cracks.'

74

CIA Protective Custody Detail — Palo Alto

'How's our boy settling in?' Assistant Director Terrance Wolf asked Special Agent Kate Linnes who was assigned lead on the Harding surveillance unit.

'He's playing by the book so far, sir,' Linnes told him.

'I'm reading you dailies and I'm not happy with him riding that stupid push bike. Can we get him a car?' Wolf asked.

'Lucas Harding doesn't drive, sir,' she said.

'Doesn't or won't?'

'He says cars add to global warming,' Linnes reported.

'They do, I guess. But having his skull crushed by a bus won't stop climate change,' Wolf announced.

'I could get him an electric car. Do I have your authorisation?'

'Sure, get the little green bastard an electric car, why not? It's only tax-payer money.' Wolf wasn't concerned, he'd bought Saudi princes Lamborghinis by the dozen for intelligence information.

Wolf read more of the transcript.

'What's this about him talking to a woman in the gym?' he asked. 'They spoke for several seconds. Have you done a run up on her?'

'We got some pictures and ran a partial face recognition, but she never looked directly into a camera. We didn't get enough point hits for an ID. We attempted to follow her, but she slipped into a busy cafe and we lost her.'

'Tradecraft?' Wolf asked.

'Can't be sure, sir.' Linnes told him. 'But she's on our list. We'll try to get more if she shows up again.'

'He appears to have a predictable work routine. Are John Carol and Kurt Hangle still in line? Any flags?'

'None, sir. They all get to the lab at about the same time. They conference, disperse, and work. At night they mostly go back to their apartments. They don't appear to speak with or meet anyone outside the group. On Wednesdays they meet at Cahoots bar for a meal and to play pool.'

'Cahoots? Is that a titty bar?' Wolf asked.

'Ah, no sir,' Linnes reassured him. 'It's just a normal bar full of tech-heads.'

'What about web activity?'

'We have real time feeds from their computers that show mostly work-related inputs. As you'd expect, lots of tech stuff, online chess, war gaming, and a bit of porn. Quite a bit of chat room flow, but our analyst says it's all nerd stuff,' she informed him.

'Okay, good.' Wolf was reassured. 'I see the apartment next to Harding was leased to an IT consultant. Has anyone had eyes on him?'

'It's a couple, sir. They're out all day. Working stiffs, who mostly get in between six p.m. to eight p.m. Cameras in the building pick them up coming and going, but their faces aren't in our databases.'

'They are in close proximity to our boy,' Wolf told her. 'Get a bug in the room and have them followed so we can put them to bed.'

At eight p.m. the next night, Mack and Ange arrived home at the apartment together. They hacked the CIA camera feeds and changed the loops, then performed a bug sweep.

Mack found two bugs and showed them to Ange. He led her into the bathroom, turning on the shower.

'At least we know how tight their grip is,' Ange told him. 'Let's go to routine one.' The couple went to the kitchen and began making a meal. They talked about their day like a regular married couple.

'I'm bushed, honey,' Ange yawned for the microphones. 'I'm off to bed.'

'Yeah, I won't be far behind you. I'm just to going to watch some Netflix.'

Mack opened his laptop and activated an anti-Wi-Fi surveillance programme. He plugged in a small black box that harmonized with the frequency of the CIA bugs and connected them to the TV. With broad smile, Mack selected a documentary titled: "The Wonders of Fungi."

That should do it, he mused.

One hundred yards down the road, a tattered blue plumber's van sat motionless. The two CIA technicians inside monitored their equipment.

'Is that it? Do people actually watch shows about fungus?' Agent Kessler asked. 'This guy has a hot wife who's going to bed, and he's watching fungus growing on shit.'

'I have a degree in science, halfway through another in forensic psychology, and I'm stuck in a van with you listening to the wonders of fungi,' Agent Brack moaned.

'That's why you joined the CIA,' Kessler told him. 'Travel the world and kill people. That bastard at The Farm may have oversold it.'

'If this gig goes longer than three days, I'm going to kill you, then myself,' Brack declared.

'Don't miss, asshole. I need the holiday.'

At precisely nine p.m., Mack watched his door open and handed Lucas a note that read that the room is bugged.

Lucas nodded. Mack pointed to a chair next to the TV and gave a sit-down motion.

Ange emerged from the bedroom wearing blue jeans with fashion rips at the thighs. She wore a white tee-shirt that failed to conceal her red bra beneath.

Lucas took a breath.

She had changed the colour of her hair to jet-black, combed back with wet-look product. She looked like a fashion cover-girl slumming it for the night.

Lucas attempted not to stare while she breezed across the room. Ange sat on the sofa opposite him and crossed her legs. Lucas glanced at her skin protruding from the rip in her jeans, then looked back to Mack.

Ange watched Lucas, assessing him. But said nothing.

Mack sat on the other side of the TV and turned up the volume, edging his chair closer toward Lucas.

'We can't underestimate the surveillance they have on you,' Mack told him quietly. 'Our next move will need to be planned to a tee.'

He gave Lucas a moment to absorb this.

'Did you talk to your team?' Ange asked.

'My guys are fully committed. They have been all along. Kurt Hangle, my electromechanical engineer, was building next gen gadgets by the age of twelve. If we can conceive it, Kurt can build it. John Carol is a particle theorist like me. We basically feed off each other when it comes to working through problems.'

'Are either of them married?' Ange asked.

'No, we all have virtually no social life. Nothing to leave behind. They are as dedicated to this project as I am.'

'As we all are.' Ange smiled at the nervous young physicist. Her smile relaxed him immediately.

'Let's eat,' she announced.

The three quietly enjoyed a simple meal of feta cheese, green olives, dolmades, and prosciutto ham. Ange sliced some crusty bread and drenched it in olive oil. Mack opened a bottle of California chardonnay, and they raised their glasses.

'Never thought I'd say this, but your local wine is not completely shit,' Ange said. M. Mack laughed in response.

Lucas shrugged, a little embarrassed. He knew very little about wine. He enjoyed the odd beer, but that was about it. Research scientists lived like monks. Fourteen hours a day working, living on canned tuna and pizza. For a special treat, he put mayonnaise on his tuna, with a drink selection of red bull or red bull extreme.

'Never mind, Lucas,' Ange purred. 'If the next year goes as planned, I'll teach you about some of the things you have been sacrificing for.'

Lucas looked at Ange. *Imagine that,* he thought to himself. *Imagine a woman like Angelina Cohen teaching him what life is all about.* He then shivered.

Mack watched Ange plying her trade. Mack's role was to own the head, while Ange owned their hearts. Not too much, though, he cautioned. The boy still must function.

'Okay,' Mack began. 'Down to business. Here's what will happen next.'

Cahoots bar was always busy on a Wednesday night, packed with tech workers who'd written one too many lines of code. Beers flowed and buffalo wings were devoured.

Lucas Harding, John Carol, and Kurt Hangle each had a beer to keep up the appearance of normality, also to calm their collective nerves. They drank some beer and ate some chicken, then they played pool. To a man, they felt the tension of waiting. Their immediate future would bring either liberation, or prison.

The clock on the wall seemed to stand still as they waited for ten p.m.

'Last chance guys,' Lucas announced. 'In fifteen minutes, we'll be fugitives. What do you say?'

'Man, I am both shitting myself and excited beyond words,' John Carol told him. 'This is the dream we had since high school. Remember, Lucas, in that stupid treehouse we built? The wireless power we collected from the TV tower?'

'That's where it started. The ghost of Nikola Tesla coming to life. What about you, Kurt?' Lucas mused.

'I spent three years in university with people saying our dream is impossible,' Kurt began. 'That it will never happen. But I've always known, in my heart, an energy capture receiver can be built. We just haven't done it yet.'

'Aren't you scared of the whole thing?' John asked. 'I mean, what if it all falls to shit?'

'We're science nerds with no real life now.' Kurt was laughing. 'How much worse could it get?'

John and Lucas were laughing too. They knew this was all or nothing.

The CIA agents in the van had viewed this scene many times.

'The boys are having a good time tonight,' Agent Brack announced.

'I'm so pleased the boys are having fun. I haven't had a proper shit in a week,' Kessler declared.

'You really fucking stink too,' Brack told him. 'Sorry, but if I can't tell you… Oh, wait one. They all got up. Must be going to the shitter.'

'Together? These nerds are fucking weird.'

'Nope, just playing pool,' Brack reported. 'Fucking assholes. I need a piss.' He opened the sliding side door and went behind a tree. It was a long luxurious piss, with the bonus of getting some fart-free air.

Then an old woman walked past with her dog.

'That's disgusting,' she told him.

Agent Brack shook badly, splashing his hands and pants, swore an appropriate curse, then re-entered the van looking for a wipe cloth.

Taking his seat, he focused his camera into the bar and found the boy's table empty. He searched the bar, then the pool table.

Nothing but unknown geeks.

'Our boys are gone!' Brack said. 'Did you see them leave?'

Kessler lifted his head from his tablet. 'Nope. They must have left. Call it in.'

Seconds earlier, the three scientists exited through the rear fire door and into the alley. At once they saw the white van and ran toward it. The doors swung open to show Mack waiting for them.

'Give me everything you own that runs on batteries,' he instructed. 'Now dump them in the bag.'

The boys complied and jumped into the van. Mack threw the bag on the ground and hit the gas.

They all heard a small explosion behind them as the destruction-bag detonated their cell phones, smart watches, and tablets in a puff of smoke.

Angelina Cohen was not with them. She was standing next to the CIA van, and she placed a small EMP (electromagnetic pulse) device on the roof.

She pressed the timer and stood back. It gave a mild bang, killing all the CIA communication devices.

As the CIA men stumbled out of the van, she shot them with a tranquilizer gun. One agent, then the other, stumbled and went down.

'Sleep well guys,' she told them.

She walked to her car and drove at the speed limit through town, then joined the 101 toward Moffatt field.

It was one a.m. before the CIA missed their agents, giving Mack's team a two-hour, forty-five minute head start.

They reached Moffatt Field and boarded a small piston powered Robertson R4 helicopter that Ange had hotwired.

'I stole it. I fly it,' she told Mack, who knew better than to argue with her.

Everyone piled in.

The R4 was designed for four people, so the chopper was cramped and overloaded. Nonetheless, Ange climbed the R4 to three thousand feet so radar could get a good look at them and flew south for ten minutes.

When they reached the Black Mountains, she descended to two hundred feet, just above the mountains, and flew southeast.

They were now lost on radar.

She skirted Sanborn Forest to avoid flying over homes and finally turned back north toward Stockton Metro Airport.

The R4 was not a big, stable, jet powered chopper, yet Ange flew it like a bird. The moonlight gave everyone a gothic, sepia-stained view of the world as they raced through the night.

'Oh shit!' Ange declared.

'What?' asked Mack.

'Heads up and hold on tight!' she yelled. 'We're about to hit a squall.'

Within thirty seconds, the flight had changed from a serene cruise to blinding rain and unpredictable wind draughts. Ange worked the full stick and rudder hard as the small chopper was shoved violently about the sky.

'It's going to be a bit bumpy for a while. Keep your seat belts tight!' Ange warned them.

John's head banged hard against his window.

'A bit bumpy, hey,' he mumbled. 'It's like being in a washing machine back here.'

The little Robertson then performed a dramatic pitch upward, then dropped fifty feet before Ange was able to haul it back in line.

Mack watched her face illuminated by the instrument lights.

'You love this shit!' he told her.

'Fuck you, cowboy!' she laughed.

Another sideways gust of wind hit the chopper, and the boys vomited in unison.

'Hey! You're going to clean my helicopter!' Ange told them.

This was followed by yet another rapid vertical heave. The boys puked again.

After another minute or so, the storm finally petered out then vanished behind them as Ange made her approach to Stockton. Everyone on board was keen to escape the vomit-chopper, as it was later called.

At one fifteen a.m., Ange crossed the airport boundary near the southwest corner and found an empty square of concrete to land.

'Let's not do that again,' Mack intoned.

'You're such a pussy,' Ange told him. 'Here, boys, take this towel and clean yourselves up. Here is some water also. Let's go, follow me.'

They muttered their thanks and followed Ange like travel weary children. They silently elevated her status to that of a bonafide Wonder Woman.

Mack had gone ahead and opened a hangar door. He found and activated a light panel and the huge blacked-out hangar slowly turned to daylight.

In the centre was a Global 5500 Learjet. The boys were shocked, and being nerds, they knew all about this plane. It had a range of some six thousand nautical miles.

'Bit of an upgrade from Ange's crappy little chopper, hey?' Mack asked them. 'Come on, get aboard! Use the bathroom to clean up and check the saloon for your new clothes. Food is in the galley.'

The boys stood there stunned.

'Move it, guys. Come on!' he called and led them onboard. Mack went into the cockpit and started the pre-flight checklist.

Ange did the safety check walk-around, inspecting the flight surfaces, tires and pulling out the external sensor bungs. She moved to the front of the plane and led Mack though a flight-surface check.

Ange then opened the rear doors of the hanger and signalled the all clear to start the engines.

Mack started engine one, then engine two and increased the power. The big jet strained against its wheel holding chocks. He powered back down to idle. They were ready to fly.

Ange then felt a tug on her arm. She spun around to find two security guards facing her.

As the noise abated, one guard was asking her what the hell was going on. By this time Mack was coming down the stairs with a clipboard full of paperwork.

'Gentlemen, good evening. How can I help you?' he asked the guards.

'What are you doing?' one of the guards asked. 'This airport is closed. There are no more flights out tonight.'

'No problem,' Mack told him. We have a special clearance. See?' He handed the guard the clipboard.

As the guard took it and started reading while Ange shot him in the neck with her dart gun.

The second guard wheeled back, going for his sidearm. Ange shot at him too. The second guard was ready for this and dived left, still going for his gun. Ange only missed once and shot him in the chest.

The guard had managed to draw his gun as he fell, firing a round into the roof.

'You're getting sloppy in your old age,' Mack told her.

Ange thought about shooting Mack too, but thought he was too heavy to carry back onboard.

'Get the wheel chocks before their pals show up,' he told her.

With the agility of a jungle cat, Ange swept under the plane pulling both chocks free and hauled them clear of the plane. She then raced aboard.

Mack was already seated in the cockpit and running the engines up again. He didn't have to worry about fuel, the plane was ready to go.

He powered up and rolled clear of the hangar. With practiced skill, he taxied to the runway, setting his flaps to fifteen percent as he went. He could see ground traffic activity leaving the security building to the east, but they were too far away to cause a problem.

He taxied directly onto the runway, planted the brakes, and spun up the engines. At one hundred percent power he released the brakes, and the plane lurched forward with the aggression of a fighter.

Ange was his co-pilot and called out the airspeed.

'Sixty knots, eighty, one hundred, one hundred twenty, N1 (point of no return), one hundred forty, rotate!'

Mack could see the security vehicles had spotted him and changed course toward him. He eased back on the yoke and the Lear left the ground like a leaf, clearing the security vehicles by several feet.

Now in flight, he raised the wheels and corrected the climb. He raised the flaps and they were already reaching two hundred and eighty knots. The Lear was a powerful plane, and Mack needed to power back his climb to seventy percent thrust.

Mack left his radios off and had disconnected the transponder. Air traffic controllers only tracked transponders, not actual aircraft. Only the military radars tracked returns.

Without air traffic guidance, Mack's main concern was colliding with another plane. To minimize this risk, he flew well away from the jet lanes.

As the jet climbed into the night, Mack set a course due west. They would fly below normal commercial jet traffic, but higher than most civil aviation. He also needed the military radar stations to get a good look at him.

The Interview

'I'm trying to count the number of felonies and FAA laws broken so far,' said Rowland Smith.

'Don't bother,' Lucas replied. 'There are way too many to count.'

'So, you're on a plane heading out to sea, to where? Let me guess, Hawaii?'

That's the big question,' Lucas said 'Mack didn't tell us the truth about our actual destination. As far as we knew we were heading for an island off South America. But that was just a ruse in case anyone got cold feet, or we were captured and forced to talk.'

'Okay, you've got me hanging, where are you going now?'

'Osaka, Japan. With a few twists and turns in between!'

'Oh, I'm sure there'll be more twists,' said Rowland but this can't work. Japan is a friend and ally of the US. Wouldn't they just hand you back?'

'They would unless a deal was already made. Mackenzie James operated on multiple levels simultaneously. "See the whole board" was his favourite saying.'

'A chess analogy,' asked Rowland.

'Exactly. He told us to "See your goal and focus on all the steps in achieving the goal. All big goals are just a series of smaller processes. Build the right ladders that connect the processes and you achieve your goal."'

'Wise man, was our Mack.'

Osaka, Japan — One Year Earlier.

Mack had been with Angelina Cohen for five years, but their relationship was not your typical suburban two kids and a dog show. Their work took them all over the globe. They managed clean energy investments and met with global players in pursuit of new opportunities.

In a world of constant motion, solar farms and hydroelectric dams in China led to wind farms in Europe. The projects spawned enough money for Mack to build a massive solar-electric ship that cleaned the oceans of plastic waste.

Sexually, they still enjoyed each other when their schedules placed them in the same city, but the pair made no unrealistic exclusivity commitments.

The Fukushima Daiichi nuclear disaster in 2011 sent tremors of fear through the Japanese government. The Americans virtually forced them to go nuclear decades earlier, even though their island chain is one of the most earthquake and tsunami prone on earth.

Seeking alternative energy sources, the Japanese Ministry of Energy commissioned a team of engineers to explore their options. In time, they met with Mackenzie

James. Angelina Cohen spoke fluent Japanese, so she flew as his wingman.

The Japanese were not happy about three things. One; Mack was an American. Two; his business partner was a woman, and three; the Japanese detested asking the Americans for help.

Their initial meeting was formal and cold. Mack expected this and acted accordingly. Ange was an ex-Mossad spy and it took more than a bunch of snotty Japanese engineers to upset her.

Over time, the Japanese learned they could trust Mack. They liked his candid and respectful manner. He showed no typical American bravado, but a quiet, deferential demeanour.

The first meeting gained little traction, yet an early bond had formed. As a reward, the Japanese paid the Americans a huge compliment by inviting Mack and Ange to dinner and drinks.

After a first-class Japanese meal, they drank sake in a gaudy karaoke bar. The singing was horrible, and the flashing lights almost induced brain seizures.

Ange could hit a note, but Mack sounded like a wounded Johnny Cash.

By one a.m., two of the younger scientists had sandwiched Ange on a sofa. One was telling her how much he loved her, reciting ancient Japanese poems of romance. The other was content to sit and drool at her.

She appeared to be enjoying herself, so Mack left her to it.

Another man, who spoke perfect English, suggested Mack should follow them upstairs.

This offer made Mack was a little nervous. The man saw Mack's reaction and laughed.

What the hell, Mack thought. You only live once.

They ended up in a cavernous saloon with a large, horseshoe shaped sofa in the centre of the room. There sat a bevy of young Japanese women in tight-fitting little dresses of various colours.

A rainbow of delights. Mack smiled.

He had had a couple more than two scotches, and wondered if they were geishas. *They can't be,* wrong *outfits, and not enough makeup, he thought to himself.*

One of the girls stood and floated toward him. She was possibly the most beautiful Asian girl he'd ever seen. A face that could sell a million Lexus's. She introduced herself as Sam Kimura.

What a great name! He played it back in his head a few times, realising he was pretty drunk.

'Hi, Sam Kimura,' he said a little too loudly. 'What's a nice girl like you doing in a place like this?' he said more quietly.

What a stupid thing to say, Mack chided himself.

'I could ask you the same thing,' Sam chided. Mack laughed. *She's fast,* he thought.

'I must tell you, Miss Kimura. I'm a little shy around pretty girls.'

'I doubt that Mr James,' she purred at him. 'You seem comfortable enough to me.'

Mack was becoming very focused on this beautiful, witty girl.

'So, let me guess,' he began. 'You're studying marine biology. Or maybe, psychology?'

'Marine biology! Why do you guess that Mr James?' She faked shock. 'Do you think I'd look good in a wetsuit? And psychology is for amateurs. I hold a master's degree in international law and finance.'

Now Mack was confused. He didn't like being drunk and confused both at the same time. He realized his feet hurt, and wondered if he could sit down.

'So, Sam, if I may call you that?' Mack attempted a recovery. 'Am I to assume you are here paying off your tuition?'

Sam Kimura giggled, using both hands to hide her mouth in mock geisha style.

'No, silly! I earn well over a million US dollars a year as an investment consultant. Why should I work here?'

Mack rocked back on his heels. He wasn't expecting that answer either, so he chose silence as his defence strategy.

'I am here for you, Mr James,' Sam's tone had changed. She was now all business. 'I am tasked to get you focused on helping Japan. We need your alternative energy experience and contacts to help Japan fix our fucking energy crisis.'

Mack was no longer smiling. Sam watched Mack deflate and giggled again. This time she did not cover her mouth.

'Come on big man, pucker up! Show me how bad you are at dancing. Ange tells me you really suck at it!'

'What the fuck just happened?' he whispered to himself.

The Interview

'Okay, I get it. Mack had already established an untouchable home for your research project in Japan,' said Rowland.

'Correct. The island off Chile was a ruse to send the CIA on a wild goose chase.'

'All that work money and risk, just for a ruse?'

'Worth every cent,' said Lucas. What you need to understand is that Mack was a student of Sun Tzu, the ancient Chinese warlord. You must never underestimate your enemy, and that subterfuge is the art of war. He also taught us that if you choose to hide, then hide in deep in the earth where you can never be found.'

'I get all that. But how the hell did you escape from America to Japan without leaving a trail?'

'That, my dear Rowland, was the trick.'

As dawn broke, the CIA Security team in California was catching up on the events of the previous night., Deputy Director Terrance Wolf was briefing CIA director, Arron Gearing.

'It took two hours before you discovered your surveillance team was down outside the bar?' Gearing asked accusingly.

'Yes, sir,' Wolf replied blandly.

'And they were shot with a nerve agent after an EMP blew out the van's comms?'

'Correct,' Wolf intoned.

'Who the hell uses EMPs and nerve agents?' Gearing was thinking hard. 'We must be looking at a foreign government here. Have you analysed the surveillance tapes?'

'We have a fresh team on that now,' Wolf told him. 'Team One has been up all night chasing these bastards.'

'The chopper they stole from Palo Alto; can you make any connection to the owner?'

'No, sir. He's a local dentist we dragged out of bed this morning. His alibi seems tight. His phone records, and bank details gave us nothing. We have checked radar tapes for the area, but shortly after take-off the chopper disappeared into the hills to the south.'

'The south?' asked Gearing.

'Shortly after, there was an event at Stockton Metropolitan airport. A large Learjet performed an unauthorized take-off. Two guards were, once again, tranquilized by what appears to be the same nerve agent used on my men.'

'Where did the Lear go?'

'That's the thing,' Wolf began. 'It flew west, directly out to sea, then passed beyond our coastal radar.'

'What's its range? Presuming it had a full tank.'

'Just short of six thousand miles.'

'Can it fly across the Pacific?' Gearing asked.

'Only just, but our aviation guys say they wouldn't attempt it. Too many variables like weather and headwinds. It will likely fly to somewhere else in the mid-Pacific for a refuelling stop.'

'That's pretty stupid,' Gearing said. 'We have military bases everywhere out there, and we know they're coming. I can't see there's much more you can do there. Hand over the clean-up to someone and get yourself to Pearl, ASAP.'

'Yes, sir,' Wolf told him.

'The President will be in a rage over this!' Gearing warned him. 'Let's put a basic story together for him so he doesn't start firing people. I want a full report on my desk in an hour. I need the who, the why, and the how. Don't fuck this up any further.'

'I understand, sir,' Wolf nodded.

'When we find these bastards, and their handlers, I want it all cleaned-up. Their plane will have disappeared over the Pacific Ocean and no bodies will be recovered,' Gearing instructed. 'Do you understand?'

'Copy, sir. It will be cleaned.'

Mack, Ange, and the boys were now two thousand miles west of the US coast and clear of coastal radars and loitering navy ships.

It was time for the next leg.

The young scientists were in fairly good shape after their night of adventure, yet everyone reacted to stress differently.

Lucas fell into a deep sleep. While John Carol and Kurt Hangle were both a little manic and couldn't stop talking. They were busy explaining frequency resonance and its potential to unlock vacuum energy to Ange, who had adopted the role of babysitter.

Ange attempted to follow their conversation, but as they explained the precept of frequency modulations and the manipulative effects on sub-atomic energy particles, she became very sleepy.

They drew diagrams and walked her through some algorithms, but it didn't help. She smiled at the enthusiastic boys and left them to it, finding a comfortable chair in the back of the plane to sleep.

Mack, too, was exhausted. Everyone had their limits and he had reached his, yet he still had work to do. It was time to change course.

He moved the autopilot dial to one hundred and eighty degrees south and the Lear gracefully dipped her left wing in compliance. With the turn complete, he checked the flight settings, navigation, and sensors. He checked fuel levels, auto tank select, internal and external temperatures. He knew there was little need for sensor de-icing. But as a professional pilot, he did it anyway.

He sat for a while, running though the list again to ensure he remembered everything. Satisfied, he went into the cabin where all was calm and peaceful. His chatty physicists had finally collapsed.

He then watched Ange sleep for a few seconds, longing to spoon in behind her. He desired the feel of her body and the smell of her hair, but he knew she was taking the next flight shift and he needed her functioning.

Mack was confident the plane could fly itself for a couple of hours. They were well beyond the authorities and flying above the weather, so he found an empty chair and fell into a fitful sleep.

In what felt like just a few seconds, a soft mouth kissed his ear. He opened his eyes to find Ange's face inches from his. She smelt like soap and toothpaste. Her soft voice was saying his name.

'Wake up, sleepyhead,' she said in her smooth husky voice.

Mack shook his head and ran his hands down his face. 'How long have I been out?'

She smiled. 'Three hours.'

He felt terrible. Ange handed him a coffee. Strong, with cream and one sugar. Perfect, as usual.

'Where are we?' he asked, guessing Ange had woken earlier and taken a shift at the controls.

'We flew one hour thirty minutes south, then one hour thirty south-east. We are now flying east toward Baja Sur, Mexico, as per our flight plan,' Ange reported in total command of the flight.

Mack smiled contentedly, knowing he could trust Ange with his life.

'We have an hour to land, and it's time for you to do your pilot stuff.' She grinned at him.

Ange was made for this world, Mack knew. Stealing planes and running from government agents was like rolling out of bed for her. Conversely, Mack was tired of this madness. He just wanted it over so the boys could start their work.

He needed to get his head in the game. The next leg was the big one, as it will set up their final getaway.

On the way to the cockpit, Lucas approached them.

'I think it's time you told us everything,' he said.

Mack could see the young man was unsure. So, he sat Lucas down, joined by John and Kurt. He took them through the stages of the plan. It was simple in its complexity.

'It's all based on subterfuge and confusion,' Mack told them. 'We must always assume the CIA will get information, and our job is to make sure that information is wrong. To keep them looking in the wrong direction.'

Mack took a swig of coffee.

'Right now,' he continued, 'We are about to land in a charming little town called Las Paz, Mexico. The CIA will have agents there to report the arrival of this plane. They will assume we either going to Mexico, or we are heading deeper into South America. By the time they have searched that part of the world, we will be long gone. It's all about buying time for you guys to complete the project.'

Lucas looked at his companions. John nodded, and Kurt smiled.

'Any questions?' Mack asked them.

Lucas scratched his head. 'Hundreds, but I trust you and Ange. We can get into the details later.'

'Good! Then if you'll excuse me, I must land this bucket of bolts.'

At one hundred miles from the coast, Mack adjusted course to Las Paz International Airport. He flipped on the Lear's transponder and radios. He set the frequencies to the Mexican air traffic control to announce his presence and ask for flight following.

At thirty miles, the air traffic controller handed Mack off to La Paz airport tower for final landing instructions.

'Here goes,' Mack told Ange. Ange kissed him on the cheek. 'For luck,' she said.

'Lear Five Seven Nine Three, Las Paz Tower, requesting a full stop landing and temporary parking on the apron,' Mack called to the tower.

'La Paz, Lear Five Seven Nine Three. Ping four four seven zero,' was the response.

'Copy, ping four four seven zero.'

Mack adjusted his transponder.

'Lear Five Seven Nine Three, I have you at ten thousand feet, thirty miles to the east. Make your course seventy for a runway one-nine approach. Descend to seven thousand and reduce speed to two hundred and twenty knots, how copy?'

'Course seventy. Make runway one-nine, descending to seven thousand and two hundred and twenty knots, Lear Five Seven Nine Three.'

'Lear, make contact when at fifteen miles.'

'Copy tower, fifteen miles,' Mack ended the conversation.

Mack and Ange knew the risk of this leg. They had given away their aircraft description via the transponder. But they needed the CIA to find the plane. The gamble was, that the CIA could not react in time to catch them.

Forty minutes later, the jet was parked and abandoned. Ange and Mack had scrubbed the plane clean of fingerprints and other identifying traces. The team made their way to a car rental kiosk, where Mack hired a Suburban, using a fake passport and license.

The team were traveling again, this time seeking rest and a good meal. They had made good their escape so far but needed to stop and revive for their final voyage.

After a short drive, they stopped at the Grand PLaa La Paz. The Grand was a much simpler hotel than its name suggested. It had a great waterfront view and plenty of sunshine. Mack and Ange got a room, and a suite for the boys to share.

They agreed to use the rest of the day sleeping and ordering room service, wanting to stay out of the public eye.

Ange had finished her shower and stood before Mack in a towel.

'I need to relax,' she told him. 'Any suggestions?' She dropped the towel.

Before he could speak, she moved in and smothered him with her still moist body.

Welcome to Mexico, Mack told himself.

The Interview

'I have to tell you; it's like you were living a Robert Ludlum novel,' said Rowland.

'We were busy people there for a while!' Lucas agreed.

'I can't imagine how angry the CIA must have been at this point. I'm pretty sure they didn't react well to being made fools of.'

'No, they did not see the humorous side at all,' Lucas confirmed. 'However, they did react as we hoped they would.'

'Well, my dear chap, we all know how the world is judging you now, so who cares? But before we get ahead of ourselves, you are still in Mexico. How did you make your final getaway?'

'It was pretty simple actually,' Lucas told him. 'Twelve hours after our Grand PLaa La Paz break, we drove south to Cabo San Lucas, on the southernmost tip of the Baja Sur.'

'I've been there,' Rowland mused. 'Not my taste of course, but each to his own.'

'Come on, Rowland!' Lucas chided. 'How could you not like it? Cabo is a playground for America's rich and famous. It also attracted more than a few international playboys, including Japanese businesspeople.'

'I see. Did you happen to meet any Japanese businesspeople per chance?' Rowland asked with one eyebrow raised.

'Yes Rowland, we did. In fact, we hitched a ride on a plane chartered by a very accommodating Japanese lady called Sam Kimura.'

'Let me guess. The charter originated somewhere in South America?'

'I think you're onto us, Rowland,' Lucas said with a huge grin 'In fact, it was a Chilean charter!'

'So, let me guess again,' Rowland said, running with the narrative. 'You boarded the Japanese chartered flight and commenced a thirteen-hour flight to Japan. How did you spend the time?'

'Let's just say it was a long time to be confined in a metal tube with two alpha women and Mackenzie James caught in the middle,' Lucas said laughing.

Carbo San Lucas is a paradise that lured some of the wealthiest people on earth to come and play. Limousines, hotels, beaches, restaurants, yachts in their marina. It was all there waiting to be enjoyed.

Our fugitives, of course, could enjoy none of it as they abandoned their car and raced into the International Airport.

The place was crowed and understaffed, as the Mexican authorities had very little interest in who was entering Mexico, and less so about who was leaving.

Mack, Ange, and the boys had changed passports again. Everyone wore large hats with sunglasses to hide their faces from the cameras, and there was no facial scanning technology.

They went through the gates and saw a man holding a sign that read: Pacific Leap. *Very humorous*, Mack thought.

The team followed the man who led them to the private jet aprons. There they boarded a big, beautiful Gulfstream G550. It was a real upgrade in size and range from the Lear, with all the modern convenances.

'I'm getting used to this jet set lifestyle,' Kurt announced, smiling ear to ear. John Carol shock his head.

'Not me, I just want to get somewhere and calm the hell down. I haven't had a decent night's sleep in two days.'

Kurt smacked him on the back. 'You're an old man John. Maybe I can find some slippers for you?'

'Oh, could you?' John replied. 'Maybe rustle up a nice cup of tea?'

A flight attendant overheard them and introduced herself as Ann. She was a slightly built Japanese lady with a pretty and patient face and the boys guessed her age as being anywhere from twenty to twenty-five.

'Can I get you gentlemen anything?' Ann asked. 'Food, or drink?'

John smiled broadly. 'Can I have some tea, please?'

'Of course,' Ann told him. John decided jet setting might work out for him after all.

For the remainder of the flight, the three scientists alternated between brainstorming, eating, and sleeping. All the while being spoilt by Ann.

Mack, Sam Kimura, and Ange went through the logistical details of the project for an hour or so, then settled into the trip.

CIA Sacramento Office

Terrance Wolf was busy liaising with Central Pacific Naval Command who were busy searching for the missing Lear.

Sorties of E2 Hawkeye radar surveillance planes crisscrossed all possible flight routes from Johnson Atoll in the south, Hawaii, and north to the Aleutian Islands. The navy didn't mind too much, they enjoyed having a real-world task to break up their routine training schedule.

On airfields in the region, F-22 fighter pilots were placed on high alert, tasked to intercept the Lear as soon as it was detected. Their orders were clear; force the plane down at Pearl or destroy it.

Wolf would have preferred ordering it to be simply shot down over the Pacific, but that would raise too many questions. After all, America didn't do that sort of thing anymore. He would have a CIA kill team do his dirty work after they landed.

As the hours passed, Wolf watched the clock and did the math. It was clear the Learjet was not flying across the Pacific Ocean. He video-linked with the senior commander in the region and ran through their options.

'The jet has a range of under six thousand miles and was last seen heading west. If it was flying to anywhere in Asia, it had to fly past us.' Wolf said.

Admiral Cal Blakley was heading the search.

'A seagull could not get through the web we have in place,' Blakley announced. 'To achieve an Asian, or even a Russian landfall to the north, the jet would need to fly at the optimum altitude and airspeed. These are a minimum of twenty-eight thousand feet and four hundred knots.'

'Yes, and as we know, they would be buffeting the Jetstream all the way. There are at least two weather fronts in either direction.'

'So, the only logical way their flight could work is a refuelling stop in Hawaii,' Blakley declared. 'All possible Central Pacific strips, and in the Aleutians, are military.'

Wolf ran his hand through his hair. He felt all his fifty-seven years as the reality of the situation hit home. He had been outwitted twice by operatives he had not yet identified. This was a clusterfuck on a monumental scale.

He excused the commander and grabbed some coffee.

Wolf then called the Sacramento Field Office. He had assigned Senior Agent Rene Zeist to command what he thought was a local clean up phase of the manhunt.

'Rene, they are not flying west,' he told her. 'What do you have?'

'We activated our flight control tower agents along the west coast of the US and Mexico. Five minutes ago, we got word from Mexico our Learjet landed at Las Paz International.'

Wolf was stunned. 'The Baja Sur in Mexico? Are you sure?'

'They flipped on their transponder, bright as a button and landed like it was all cool and normal,' Zeist told him.

Wolf considered this strange revelation for a moment. 'They must have known the transponder would announce to the world who they were,' he said. 'These people must have the resources to be able to switch on a fake unit if they wanted to. Did they want us to know it was them? From the Baja Sur, they could fly anywhere in the Americas.'

'When exactly did they land?' Wolf asked.

'Six hours ago.'

Wolf was turning red. 'Six fucking hours! Why the info lag?'

'Sir. We have limited resources in that part of Mexico,' Zeist reminded him. 'Our man on the Sur is based in Tijuana. It took him six hours to get the tower logs. As you know there are hundreds of...'

'I know this, Rene!' Wolf knew he was losing his grip. 'But we are the fucking CIA and it still took six hours to find a plane in our own backyard!'

'Sir, we have another problem,' Zeist continued. 'Our agent is flying to Las Paz as we speak. He contacted the local police, but they aren't cooperating at this point. The only thing we know is the Lear is still parked at the airport. We may need State Department intervention.'

Wolf dumped his coffee in the sink. It was not helping anymore and he took a huge swig of water instead.

'Looks like they dumped the Lear and have no doubt sanitized it. Best guess, Rene. Where are they going?'

'Best guess?' Zeist was thinking hard. 'If it were me, I'd be on the next flight out of Mexico. Logically, that means heading south.'

'South is a pretty big place,' Wolf told her. 'You'll need IDs on every hire car, boat, and everything with wings or rotors that left La Paz in the past eight hours. You have a lot of leg work to do. If they're airborne they'll be four hundred miles away and counting.'

Rene Zeist already knew the enormity of her challenge. 'Yes, sir. Once we have identified the targets, we can start our search.'

'I will have State work on getting you cooperation with their CAA guys,' Wolf assured her. 'In the meantime, I need you to bribe, threaten, or by any other means, get the video from every camera between the parked Lear to the airport.

'I'll have my tech team hacking the ground camera sites while I'm in the air,' she told him.

'Good, those faces are everything. Once we can see them, the face recognition techs can identify them,' Wolf said. 'You'll need at least fifty agents on the Sur in three hours. Split them up from Tijuana to Cabo San Lucas.'

Being the veteran he was, Wolf ran through the drill like a chef reciting an old recipe.

'I want a fast-response team of five, armed in full tactical kit. Get a command centre up and running in La Paz. There's no room for an operation like that at Cabo.

Use one of our unmarked C-130s from McClellan,' Wolf instructed.

'Tac team and command centre, copy.'

'Brief me one hour after you land. Search Cabo, but it's ninety percent they are already flying to, or are already hiding somewhere, in South America. That's the focus of your search. Copy?'

'Copy, sir,' Zeist replied.

Wolf thought for a moment. *What have I forgotten?* he asked himself. His brain was pure fog after thirty-six hours of no sleep.

'Know this, Zeist,' Wolf told her. 'Our three little bears and their handlers have been completely unpredictable so far, so assume nothing. In fact, get a Langley Red Team activated. I want some big brain hypotheses going.'

'Copy, sir,' Zeist replied, quietly wishing Wolf would stop talking so she could get to work.

You're my point guy on this,' Wolf told her. 'It's a career moment for you, so don't fuck up.'

Don't fuck it up, Zeist mused. *A typical CIA motivational line.*

'Yes, sir. I'll get them.'

Zeist checked, and rechecked, her notes. She closed her eyes and indulged herself with two deep breaths. *You can do this, girlfriend*, she told herself.

Then she hit the phones, commencing two days' work that needed to be done in just three hours.

Still in Hawaii, Wolf ran through the Zeist conversation in his head, then called out to his aide again.

'Get me the director, right now. Looks like we have tracked our three little bears.'

The Japanese Gulfstream G550

The getaway team was now flying toward Hawaii in a high-speed jet the authorities had absolutely no interest in.

By a twist of fate, they virtually crossed flight paths with Terrance Wolf who was returning to the US as he lay twitching in a fitful slumber.

After nearly four hours in the air, Mack and the team had had their power naps of varying lengths. The boys were showered, fed, and issued brand new clothes, and powerful air-gap laptops.

Ange had purchased the clothes from designer stores and the boys were not amused. Their standard apparel consisted of jeans, hoodies, and sneakers.

When Ange was done, they squirmed and scratched in designer label collared shirts, chinos, and Italian loafers.

'What the hell are these?' Lucas asked. 'Some kind of catwalk shoes? Where are the socks?'

Sam and Ange laughed. They enjoyed the try-ons, giving the boys huge encouragement and compliments.

It took the boys several minutes to acclimatize to all the female attention, but they adapted quickly and began to enjoy it.

Mack was finally able to relax. He knew their getaway was secure for one simple reason; they were still flying, and there were no American fighter planes on their wing tips.

As the sun began to set, he decided the team needed to unwind and have a little fun.

He pulled out his phone, blue-toothing his favourite rap song. Seconds later, everyone was singing along to Cypress Hill's; "Insane in the Brain".

Their flight attendant, Ann, didn't go for rap, and tried to ignore it. She was kept busy with pouring drink orders anyway. Mack and Ange had heavy-pour gin and tonics. Sam went for a fine New Zealand Pinot Noir, while the boys' ordered bourbon and cokes.

Music, drinks, snacks, and laughter filled the cabin as they celebrated their victory over oppression, as their adventure was now coined. They took turns retelling their experiences.

They recited the cramped helicopter ride through the storm. Ange shooting the airport guards with a tranquilizer gun also got a strong mention.

When Mack reminded them that Ange had missed one, she punched his arm. 'Who can guess Ange's favourite nickname?' Mack asked. 'It's Angie-baby!' Everyone liked that and a chorus of 'Angie-Baby' went up around the plane.

'Next person to say that name; I'll break your fucking finger.' Ange levelled her eyes at them.

Everyone laughed again. She grabbed Mack's hand and started bending his index finger.

They all laughed louder, to a chant of, 'Go! Go! Go!' while Mack yelled in pain. As the party matured, the cabin lights were dimmed. Sam and Ange were dancing to "Champagne Affection" while the guys enjoyed the show. Finally, they joined in.

Even Mack got up to dance, exposing everyone to his weird dance skills-or lack of. Eventually Ange, Mack and Sam collapsed on the big, padded sofa. More drinks arrived.

'Tell me, how did you guys' team up?' Sam asked, feeling lightheaded and very fine.

Mack looked at Ange, and she nodded her permission to reveal their story.

'We first met at a solar farm in Israel,' Mack began. 'Ange was working for the government.'

'Oh God!' Ange chided him. 'You're a hopeless storyteller.'

Mack threw his arms up in surrender.

'Okay, so, I worked for Israeli intelligence at the time. I was assigned to monitor the Americans. You know, to make sure they weren't all spies. Anyway, one thing led to another, and we got together.'

Sam shook her head. 'Oh, come on. There's more to it than that.'

Mack took over. 'After the solar farm, Ange and I met again in Tel Aviv. We had lunch, and she told me her story.'

Mack checked with Ange again. 'Can I tell it?'

'Sure, why not,' she conceded.

Ange took a long swig from her glass, moving her head to the music.

'Ange was working for her government somewhere in the Middle East,' Mack told Sam. 'That part is still secret. Anyway, she was captured and arrested.'

Sam viewed Ange with sympathetic sadness in her eyes.

'Really?' she asked.

Ange looked at her. She could see Sam's pretty face was sad with empathy, so she gave her a small smile.

'Ange was eventually returned to Israel as part of a prisoner swap,' Mack continued. 'But her cover was blown, and she was now on the shared database throughout the Middle East. Hamas even put out a sizable contract on her.'

'I'm going for a piss,' Ange announced.

She got up to leave, leaning over Mack, whispering in his ear. Mack nodded.

'If you don't want to say anymore, I understand,' Sam told them.

'No, it's okay,' Mack told her. 'Bottom line; Ange knew the only work for her in the security services was domestic, non-undercover, and that Hamas would eventually try to kill her. The thought of being a glorified babysitter bored her to death.'

Sam considered this. 'Makes sense,' she said.

Ange had returned, flopped heavily onto the couch, and finished her beer.

'So, I made her an offer,' Mack continued. 'Work for me as my fixer, security, and right-hand man. The work we do requires a lot of nuance, and her tactical brain has saved my bacon more than once.'

'Do you ever stop talking?' Ange asked him, making Sam laugh.

'Be nice,' Mack retorted. 'She's a cranky drunk.'

Ange put him in a headlock until he tapped out. Sam laughed some more.

'Okay, storytime is over!' Ange declared. 'Mack, I need to speak privately.'

Mack knew what that meant and jumped to his feet, following her into the sleeping cabin. Ange had a very specific method for relaxing. It involved a combination of intimate, tender closeness, and wild animal lust.

Three hours later Ange woke in a panic. She was covered in sweat and her heart was pounding.

'Nightmare?' Mack asked.

'Always,' she told him. They had become a part of her life now. Mack knew it was another flashback from her capture and time in the Syrian prison.

'I'm getting a water,' she said quietly. 'Want one?'

'Yes, thanks.'

He lay back on the bed and recounted her life story. Ange had experienced more grief and hardship than any person he'd known. But to know her, you could never tell.

She had maintained her humour and wit, along with genuine positivity in all things. But just behind the smiles, her eyes held the secrets of her past.

'It's funny the things you remember,' Ange once mused, as she told Mack her story so many years ago.

The dry, dusty heat. The bright summer sun. The sound the breeze makes as it flutters through the date palm fronds. She even recalled the ravens calling to each other from their perches along the street.

Angelina Cohen was eleven years old when she decided to become a soldier for Israel. She was there in the settlements as rockets exploded into people's homes and the bombs exploded on the buses.

Her strongest memory was on Yom Kippur many years ago, a holy day in the Jewish Calendar. As Ange explained to Mack; it's a day of forgiveness of the sins of others and one's own sins against God.

On this day, the town's people were happy as they made their way to temple. Her mother was holding her hand singing an old Hebrew song that celebrated the day.

Ange could see her fellow worshippers gathered at the foot of the temple stairs. Her friends waved to Ange as she and her mother approached.

Ange could not remember seeing the old grey car parked in front of the church, nor the man who got out yelling an Arabic prayer. But she did remember a bright flash of light and the sensation of flying backward through the air.

On that day, Ange lost her mother and many of her closest friends. She was fortunate in being so young. Her young body was supple enough to survive the force of the blast. Her mother, who was one pace closer to the explosion, took the full impact.

Yet Ange remained in hospital for a very long time.

Her father was in the army at that time and was at her bedside when she woke. She could see the tear tracks on his face and the defeat in his eyes. Ange had never seen her father look this way, and although being very young, knew her mother was dead.

Angelina Cohen was set on a path. A path that led her all the way through university, military training, and into the elite special forces.

She spent several years patrolling the mountainous desert wastelands with seventy pounds of kit strapped to her back.

While on patrol, she lived on dried biscuit, dates, and drank fetid water. Her bed, more often than not, was a ditch, where she survived on two hours sleep per day.

Her training included making battle plans and leading men into night operations with only her rifle, grenades, and a compass.

At any time, her instructors would appear from the blackness of night and attack her. There she defended herself in unarmed combat. Her instructors showed no mercy for the fact she was a woman.

Ange would awake in the base hospital having her nose realigned, bones set, and ribs strapped.

After three or four of these attacks, Ange knew she must learn how to defend herself or die. She vowed her male instructors would never volunteer to attack her again.

On the next night, they sent three men to grab her. Waiting in the dark like a feral animal, Ange was ready for them. She leapt from cover and grabbed one of her attackers in a fatal headlock, choking him hard until he went limp.

Using his body as a shield, she kicked and punched the remaining two. The toe of her boot connected with the second attacker's throat, and he went down.

Now it was one-on-one.

Her attacker lunged at her. Even in the pitch black of the desert night, Ange could see he was a big boy. Big and fast.

She sidestepped the attack, but his fist caught the side of her face and she spun backward to the ground. The attacker moved in and kicked her twice in the side, then stood back and laughed.

'A fucking woman!' he said in a booming voice. 'You think you can…'

His delay was a fatal mistake.

Ange swung both of her legs around and smashed her right boot into his exposed knee. She found out later, the soldier's knee was shattered into six pieces, and he was retired from the army.

The Israeli special forces are a hard playground, and many of the men wanted revenge. But after two more hospitalisations, the army ordered a cessation of the night attacks. They could not afford to lose good men at this rate.

During this time, a man named Beriah watched her progress closely.

Ange had submitted several applications to the highly selective Israeli intelligence service, and Beriah was assigned to her case. Beriah was looking for four principal qualities, unquestioning loyalty, high motivation, extraordinary toughness, and intelligence.

Angelina Cohen had the motivation, no question there. She had proven her ability to sustain physical stress without complaint, and her university grades were high, specifically in languages.

Beriah was a conflicted man. He knew his job was both angel and devil. He selected the very best young people Israel produced. He gave them years of training, then sent them into the lion's den to die.

He consoled himself with the knowledge that without its highly efficient spy network, Israel would have been destroyed by her enemies who both outnumbered and surrounded them.

He met monthly with the special forces' commander; a man named Boaz.

Boaz was a war veteran who believed in the old adage that how you train is how you fight. He trained his people as though Israel was at war.

'I want her hard, not ruined,' Beriah told Boaz.

'Listen to me, old man,' Boaz retorted. 'I have trained thousands of these people. I know how far I can push them.'

'That may be so, but let me tell you…' Beriah leaned in. 'I need her tough and pretty. If you keep breaking her face, what good will she be as a spy then, can you tell me that?'

Boaz hated these old Mossad recruiters. They came onto his base whenever they wanted and fucked everything up. He spends months or even years training the best soldiers, then Mossad just plucks then away.

'You do realize we are on the same side; do you know that?' Beriah attempted to console the man. 'One good spy can do more damage to our enemies than a whole company of your soldiers.'

Boaz knew this was the truth, but it did not make him feel any better. He stared at Beriah for a few more seconds, knowing he had no choice.

'Okay, fuck you, old man. You can have her.'

'I want her now, before you break her nose again,' Beriah told him.

Boaz shared a few well-chosen obscenities with Beriah, then called for his clerk to get the fucking girl.

Minutes later, Ange was led to a base interview room. The walls were faded white with more than one randomly placed spatter stain that she could only assume was blood. In the centre of the room was a table and two chairs. Beriah was sitting on one of the chairs. He introduced himself and invited her to sit.

Ange had just returned from two weeks in the desert. Her body weight had dropped to one hundred pounds, and she had a suspected concussion that was not yet medically diagnosed, let alone treated.

Beriah sighed sadly and smiled at the girl. *What a mess you are,* he mused. He knew her file back to front. He was fully aware of what this young woman had lost and now sacrificed for Israel. A lifetime of hard work, pain, and struggle for the cause. He hoped she was now ready for the final step.

Ange viewed this small, simple looking man dressed in a white short-sleeved shirt and old grey trousers. She assumed he was some kind of administrator. *Are they trying to fuck with my pay again?* she thought to herself.

'What do you want?' she asked Beriah curtly.

At this point she was well past the capacity for either manners or respectful conversation.

'It's not what I want,' Beriah began. 'The question is, what do you want?'

Ange stared back at the old man.

'What the fuck are you talking about?' she snapped at him. 'Look, I need food, a bath, and a doctor. So, can you hurry this up?'

Beriah smiled at the girl again, while Ange snarled back at him. Beriah sat back in his chair and smoothed back his hair.

'Okay. Out of respect for your current condition, I'll make this fast and dirty. You have been reassigned to the Israeli security services. Go now and get your food, then see the doctor. I will be here at six a.m. to pick you up. By then I hope your mood has improved.'

But Beriah did not pick her up the next day.

Her doctors said her concussion was worse than normal. Her ribs were broken, and her body weight was dangerously low.

'We're sending her to the army rest centre near Tel Aviv,' the doctor told Beriah.

'How long will this take?' he asked.

'It will take as long as it takes,' the doctor told him. 'Don't worry, you'll have plenty of time to get her killed on some suicide mission when she's healthy again.'

Beriah blandly stared at the doctor. *This is what they think I do*, he mused.

By day seven of rest and good food, Ange had gained ten pounds and felt almost human again. Her ribs only hurt when she coughed, and there was nothing they could do about her nose. The doctors would fix that later in a series of painful operations.

She found her best supermarket dress, brushed her hair, and applied some rudimentary makeup. She then caught a taxi to the Mossad training school.

Two years later she was naked, chained upside down and being beaten against the blood-soaked wall of a Syrian prison. This happened every day for two months.

Every day the guards told her that she would be hung in the market square. "Did you know they leave your body hanging for three days after you're dead? Did you know that?"

Ange, in fact, did know that. Then they beat her again. Not for information, she was well past ever giving that up.

They beat her for fun. They tore out her fingernails for fun. They half drowned her in water pails for fun.

The Interview

'Let me get this straight,' Rowland Smith began. 'You led the CIA on a wild goose chase across the Pacific. But you were not heading West, you changed course to the South to Mexico. You then teamed-up with the Japanese government and flew West again, partying your way across the pacific?'

'Come now, Rowland, be fair!' Lucas pleaded. 'It wasn't all a party. We still got some work done. Mack had extra oxygen pumped into the cabin the next day and we were fine.'

'I feel sorry for your flight attendant Ann. Sounds like she did all the work,' Rowland told him.

'That's not all,' Lucas beamed. 'She gave me her phone number! But it was some time before I could call her, obviously.'

'I can imagine. Did you finally call her?' Rowland asked.

'I did, and we're having dinner next time she's in the US.'

'Well done! Now tell us about Osaka.'

At the mention of Osaka, Lucas Harding bowed his head and stared at his shoes. Everyone could see the joy leave his face.

'I think we need to take a commercial break,' Rowland Smith announced.

When the cameras were off, Rowland turned back to Lucas.

'I know this is the tough part,' he said gently. 'Will you be okay?'

'I'll never be okay,' Lucas told him. 'But I'll get through it.'

Rowland smiled at the younger man and touched his shoulder.

'Good man,' he told him.

As the Gulfstream approached Japanese airspace, the boys grabbed window seats. Unfortunately, all they could see was thick, green forest.

'Trees,' Kurt reported blandly. He was hoping to see a great Japanese city. But that wasn't possible, as they were, in fact, north of Osaka where minutes later the jet touched down at an unused Japanese self-defence military airfield. The team was issued large white raincoats and instructed to use them as head covers when they disembarked. Lucas looked at Mack enquiringly.

'Satellites,' Mack told him and pointed to the sky.

Lucas nodded and quickly covered his head.

Two white vans sat on the flight apron with their engines running. Once everyone boarded, they sped off without delay, to a hangar complex toward the northern end of the airbase.

Angelina Cohen Goes Home

Ange knew her role in delivering the scientists was over. Her commitment to Mack was fulfilled, and she was not one to hover without a specific task to do.

She was now free to complete a personal task that was well overdue. For far too long she had been haunted by her capture and torture in Syria. What they did to her went far beyond rational prisoner treatment.

The anger inside her was now distilled and concentrated into a powerful desire for retribution. Her captors needed to bleed and experience pain, then be eradicated from her existence.

Ange planned her revenge.

She told Mack she needed to go back to Israel to visit her father. Which was true enough.

Three days later Ange landed at Haifa's U Michaeli International Airport, and her father was there to meet her.

After many kisses and hugs, the pair drove back to the old family home. At once, Ange could feel the presence of her mother. Her father had never remarried, and all her old things, including her photos were still in place.

Ange viewed her father as they drank tea and ate buttered bread. He was long retired now, but the years in the army had instilled the discipline to stay fit. He still looked strong and able, with just a little roundness in the middle.

'So, Angelina. What brings you home to me?' Alatan Cohen asked his daughter. Ange sipped her tea.

'I haven't seen you in so long, Pappa,' she replied. 'Does a daughter need a reason to see her old dad?'

Alatan looked sceptical.

'I wanted to see you again sooner,' Ange continued. 'But I've been working hard lately. Now I get to see you again and to recharge my batteries.'

Alatan was going to have to accept this for now, smiled at her.

'This will always be your home, Angelina. The spirit of your mother is still here, did you know that? I can feel her here with me sometimes.'

He looked up at her picture on the mantle.

'You are as beautiful now as she was.' Alatan smiled again.

His words caused Ange's eyes to mist, and a heavy tear rolled down her cheek. She didn't want to lose it, so she left it there.

Over the next few days, Ange and Alatan enjoyed long lunches by the sea and took walks on the beach. They went to the cinema and the museum, enjoying their time together.

Alatan volunteered as a counsellor for army veterans, spending four days each week at the base. Ange used this time for training. She went to the gym and worked on her strength.

She looked up a few of her old army buddies and joined in their hand-to-hand training sessions. They knew how she used to train and asked her politely not to hurt anyone.

'Remember, you motherfuckers,' the instructor told them. 'Fight hard, but no broken bones, okay?'

On alternating days, Ange strapped on a forty-pound backpack and ran up the nearby desert mountains until she had thoroughly exhausted herself.

One month later, Alatan finished his supper and looked at the girl.

'What are you training so hard for?' Alatan asked. 'Look at you! You look ready for a prize fight!'

Ange stopped eating.

'What do you mean, Pappa?' she asked.

'Come on, girl. You can't fool your old pappa. I know you are training yourself. Your backpack is full of rocks, and I'm told you are doing fight training. You are getting ready for something.'

'Oh, it's nothing special,' Ange casually replied with a dismissive wave of her hand. 'Mackenzie James wants me to provide security for a trip he has planned.'

'That man will get you killed one day. Do you know that? Always going into third world countries looking for trouble.'

'Oh, Pappa!' Ange grinned at her worried father. 'The work is not really that dangerous. Mack mostly uses me as an interpreter. Besides, the money will come in handy someday. You wait and see.'

'You are not getting any younger, Angelina,' Alatan warned her. 'When are you going to stop all this running around and maybe meet a boy? A nice Israeli boy and settle down?'

The sadness behind this question was very real for her. The truth was sadder still. Ange knew that living a full-time domestic life would kill her. After a lifetime of adrenaline and excitement, how could she ever become a happy domestic wife? Let alone a mother.

Ange knew she was damaged goods. Her fate was sealed the day she watched her mother blown to pieces standing right beside her.

'Perhaps one day, Pappa,' Ange told him. 'But not yet. I have one more job to do.'

Alatan heard the edge in her voice and knew she would be leaving him again soon. He wanted to stop her, to make her consider her options. But he also knew Ange. She had a lion inside her, and the lion was not ready to sleep.

'Yes, Angelina, perhaps one day. Just remember, you are always part of my heart and I'll be right here when you need to rest.'

'Enough of this mushy shit, Pappa!' Ange changed her tone. 'Let's drink some wine and put on the radio. You get so serious sometimes, Pappa. Did you know that?'

They both laughed, drank wine, and listened to music. It was a good night in the Cohen home.

The next day when Alatan returned home, Angelina was gone. Her room was spotless, as though she was never there.

Her flight from Haifa took her across the Mediterranean to Konya, Turkey. From the airport she grabbed a taxi to Topraklik Street, across the road from the park, and near the centre of town.

Ange loved Turkey. She loved the buildings, the people, and the smell of markets infusing the air with aromas of exotic spices. The country had all the old-world wonders of an ancient Arabic city, without all the extreme religious rules and restrictions.

She entered the apartment she kept above the local shops and quickly opened the windows to let the place breath. It had been over a year since she had been here, and it smelt sour.

She did a quick clean up to remove the dust and went downstairs to buy food and wine.

On her return, she went to the second bedroom and moved a heavy cabinet, pulling back a square of carpet to reveal a metal lockbox.

She opened the box and removed her Turkish passport along with a leatherbound folder containing travel and certification documents, including a permission to trade letter signed by the Syrian authorities.

She opened the wardrobe and selected the clothes she would need, packing them into a suitcase a Turkish businesswoman would likely travel with. Ange was now a jewellery shop owner, preparing for a buying trip to Syria.

Ange never travelled with weapons. She knew being caught with a weapon at airport customs, or a roadblock, was suicide. Besides, for the job she had planned, guns were not needed.

It was mid-afternoon when she left the apartment. She went to the bank where she topped up her credit cards with cash, then shopped for the remainder of items she would need for her trip.

Returning to the apartment she sat and closed her eyes, beginning her mental process of visualising the mission. She ran through her range of planned scenarios, and possible unplanned events.

All done! Time to relax, she told herself.

Ange took a long hot shower and indulged herself with a short nap.

As night fell, Ange realized she was still agitated. She was desperate for sexual release, and considered helping herself, but knew she needed more. She needed physical contact.

Ange had experienced these feelings regularly before major operations. She had an itch that needed scratching, so she decided to scratch it. She put on her tight blue jeans and a white top that emphasized her breasts. She applied red lipstick, brushed her long black hair, and ruffled it to frame her face.

Ange checked her appearance in the mirror and gave herself a cheeky smile. Two blocks closer to town, Ange found a lively little bar. She took a stool and ordered a martini; dirty, no olive.

Turkey is a Muslim country, yet in the cities, a single girl having a drink was not frowned upon. In fact, two fit-looking young Turkish men at a nearby table thought it was wonderful.

She glanced at the boys and gave the briefest of smiles, then looked away. *Hooked!* she mused.

After a few minutes, one of the men worked up the courage to go over to her and introduce himself. He invited Ange to join them at the table where they talked about the little things for a while until Ange asked them where they lived and would they show her.

'I hope you something to drink there?' Ange asked him. 'A girl can get very thirsty, you know.'

The men smiled and nodded enthusiastically.

Ange was escorted by the men back to a nice city apartment. They enjoyed a drink of spiced rum and smoked some hashish. They had a good selection of western music, so Ange danced for them.

She complained it was very hot and started to remove clothing. First her light jacket, then tantalizingly removed her top.

The men watched her breasts move and sway under a red bra that was half a size too small for its original purpose.

Ange kicked off her shoes and swayed her perfectly honed bottom and hips toward the boys. She then popped the top button on her jeans.

'Can you boys help me with my zipper?' she asked them.

An hour later, after much frantic thrusting and moaning, Ange said her goodbyes. She left the men stunned, naked, and sweating.

I am a slut, she told herself and laughed, feeling no more tension. She was now ready to kill a fucking rat.

Osaka, Japan

Mack loved the science of particle physics on many levels. To him, it was more than electrons, neutrons, quarks, photons, and neutrinos; the science of particle physics was a human metaphor.

In Mack's mind, the level at which humans interact with subatomic particles and the quantum energy fields was the subtext denoting our advancement as a species.

The closer humans came to accessing pure energy from these fields, the closer we are to enlightenment. A world that ran on light energy would become free of corporate and political corruption.

Poverty would be eliminated. Populist politicians and giant energy companies would have no place in a world in harmony with the power of the universe.

Mack knew the entire global structure of economic capitalism would change forever.

'We are on the brink,' Mack told Dr Haru Takahashi. 'What happens here in the next year will change everything.'

Haru was the leader of the Japanese research team. His people were assigned to assist Lucas, John and Kurt build their research facility and conduct peer reviews for their work.

Haru spoke perfect English, having studied at MIT and Caltech.

As the plans were revealed to him, Haru understood immediately the direction Mack's team wanted to go.

'Do you think this energy is truly accessible, then able to be harnessed in a controllable manner?' Haru asked Mack.

'I have already seen it,' Mack told him simply.

Haru Takahashi was aware that Mack had observed a light-energy UAP up close. He was also aware scientists over the decades had declared they had broken the code, then mysteriously died or abandoned their research.

'I know they will do it,' Mack told Haru. 'These boys started this work while they were still in high school. As Sun Tzu tells us, every battle is won or lost before it is ever fought. These boys have already won the battle. Now it's time to grind it out and build the thing.'

'You know Sun Tzu?' Haru looked at him.

'I know some,' Mack said simply.

Haru smiled at Mack and nodded. The two men stood quietly and watched their younger charges go about their work.

This generation of young men and women were not burdened with the concept of failure limitations, Haru knew. They were bold in their assumptions and creative in developing applied solutions.

'Zero-point energy, or vacuum energy, is trapped in a balance of negative and positive electromagnetic forces. Here the energy fields cancel each other out,' Lucas was addressing the latest crop of Japanese engineers.

'To access this energy,' he continued. 'We will use resonance vibration frequencies to unbalance the energy fields and draw out the energy trapped within.'

The engineers were captivated. For many of them, this was the opportunity of a lifetime.

'This project is hinged on finding the right frequencies to match the charged particles, then overload and alter the energy field balance.'

We will discover these frequencies and the sequence in which to apply them.'

'How long do you predict the research will take?' Haru asked Mack.

Mack shook his head. 'It will take two months, two years, or the rest of our lives.'

Haru was silent.

'We are attempting to trick the one true power of the universe to give up her secrets,' Mack told him.

'And our greatest threat is the American government,' Mack told him. 'They are owned by Big Energy and money is their god. They will try to kill us if we are discovered.'

Haru nodded solemnly.

'I will be standing right beside you!' Haru told him. 'I'd better not tell my wife or my insurance company.'

The two men laughed at the dark joke.

Aleppo, Syria

At nine a.m. the next day, Ange took a flight from Konya to Aleppo. She knew the most dangerous stage of her plan was getting through airport security.

Wearing her most demure faded-tan outfit, and a full headscarf, the Syrian customs soldier still greeted her with pure disgust.

He hated all Turks and he abhorred women. Now he viewed a woman who travels without a male escort!

'Papers!' the soldier yelled. He was a massive man, sporting a three-day growth and tight-fitting blue uniform with sweat stains under the arms.

His black hair was slick with either oil or filth, Ange could not tell. The man had not bathed for some time, based on his sour body odour.

Ange had passed through Arab nation airports many times. She knew success was based on her voice tones and body language. She kept her head down and handed over her passport and travel documents.

The soldier grunted at her. 'What do you want in Syria?'

'To buy beautiful Syrian jewellery, sir,' Ange told him.

'What do you want it for?' he asked.

'To sell in my shop in Konya,' Ange said quietly.

The soldier grunted again. Grunting was his favourite sound and he practiced it often. He hated Ange as a Turk. He hated her more that she travelled alone. Now, being a businesswoman, she was pure heresy.

'Access to Syria denied!' the soldier yelled. 'Wait over there.'

He pointed to a roped off holding area and raised his arm to stamp her papers.

'Sir! Please wait,' Ange begged. 'I have a letter from your government.' The soldier turned red.

'What!' he yelled.

'I have a permission to trade in Syria letter from your government,' she implored.

The soldier snorted. 'Give it to me!'

Ange handed him the letter. He snatched it from her hand and read it. He then read it again.

'Fuck some cheese,' he muttered.

He put away the red stamp, then with great malevolence stamped Ange's travel papers with a blue stamp.

'Yalla! Move away!' he yelled at her. 'Next!'

Ange shuffled off, following the airport exit sign, and entered the city of Aleppo.

Without delay, she made her way to a car hire kiosk, where after much negotiation, and a criminal amount of overcharging, she was handed the keys to an old Mercedes saloon. As she approached the car she performed a walk-around to assess the tyres. They were well-worn, but she guessed they would do the job. She then checked the oil and the radiator coolant.

Both were down but would have to do.

The car started on the second try, and she sat listening to the engine. After it warmed up, the car ran without too many knocks and clunks. She checked the fuel and drove off the lot.

Ange took the main highway west and into the city. The traffic was heavy, and it took forty-five minutes to reach the Riga Hotel. It was easy to find, being straight off the main highway.

She parked in one of the parking bays and gave the keys to the valet.

She handed the man fifty US dollars. Essentially a week's wages, which he accepted with a smile.

'Park it close by, please,' she told him.
The valet nodded happily. He was young and full of bounce, sporting his crisp fifty-dollar bill.

The Riga wasn't the highest rated hotel in Aleppo, but it was a typical stay for a foreign merchandise buyer. Ange knew all the foreign hotels were watched by the Syrian secret police, so it didn't really matter which hotel she chose.

She handed the desk clerk a second fake passport, as she would not be coming back to collect it.

Now in her room, Ange showered and dressed in a black one-piece bodysuit, then laced on heavy steel-capped boots. She ordered a room service steak, insisting it be delivered with a good steak knife.

Waiting for her meal, Ange put herself through a series of limbering up exercises. She found yoga poses worked very well in preparing for combat. She then ripped through fifty push-ups and twenty burpees, until she felt ready and focused.

When her steak arrived, she ate half without tasting it.

She bound the handle of the knife with nonslip military tape, then put it and the tape into her bag. She checked the room to ensure only her original travel clothes remained.

She tied back her hair into a ponytail and donned a shapeless shoulder-to-feet grey smock. The final touch was an old pale blue head scarf.

She looked in the mirror and saw a completely forgettable Arab female staring back at her.

Before Ange departed Israel, she had met with an old friend in Mossad, and learned the guard who held Angelina Cohen was a man called Alzuhur Ahmed.

A congruent opportunity was presented to Ange. Kill Alzuhur and her need for retribution would be met. At the same time Israel would be sending a strong message to the Syrian Government.

She was given the green light to go after him.

There was one proviso; if she was caught, the Israeli government could not save her. She would be disavowed and left to die in a Syrian prison.

Ange considered the offer and agreed immediately. She committed that, should it come to that, she would not be taken alive.

The Mossad man was satisfied and handed her a dossier.

Four Fifteen P.M., Local Time

Ange left the hotel and drove to the satellite city of Sheikh Najjar, parking in the lot of the Khaled Mohamed Bread Company.

At 5.05, a woman exited the building and made her way past Ange, and on toward her car.

Ange checked her against the photograph in the dossier. She confirmed it was the wife of Alzuhur Ahmed.

Ange pretended to study her phone as the woman drove out past her and onto the road. Ange started her car and followed the woman at a safe distance.

The woman led Ange through the suburbs of Sheikh Najjar until she parked in the driveway of a nondescript plasterboard house. Ange pulled her car over some two hundred feet away.

Ange watched the woman exited her car and enter the house.

As the sun began to set, Ange made her move. She exited her car and looked up and down the street. People were moving about but no one showed an interest in her. Clutching her bag, she made her way to the house and knocked on the door.

The door opened and Ange punched the woman in the face, sending her careening backwards, landing hard on the tile flooring.

Ange knew there were no other people living in the house. The children were grown up and living elsewhere. Ange closed the door and prepared herself for the next phase.

Ange secured Alzuhur's wife to a chair and searched the house. She found two handguns: a .45 automatic, and a revolver. She would keep the revolver as a backup weapon but could not trust the reliability of the automatic, so she hid it under the bed.

Ange now had a long wait for her prey. She used the time to meditate, then watched some Syrian television. She stared vacantly at the heavily edited and lip-synced version of Friends. She then watched some Syrian news.

Nine Fifteen P.M.

A twin beam of lights flashed into the loungeroom, and a car stopped in the driveway.

Ange heard heavy boot steps approach the front door and a rattle of keys.

The door swung open and much to the surprise of Alzuhur Ahmed, his wife sat facing the door bound to a chair. The blood from her broken nose smeared across her face.

The woman attempted a muffled warning, but it was too late.

From behind the opened door, Ange punched Alzuhur in the back of the neck and he collapsed like a bag of old potatoes.

When Alzuhur came around, his first cognition was that he couldn't move.

Ange had taped his arms and feet together, then bound his arms and feet behind his back. She had also gagged him.

She had removed her grey dress and headscarf. Now dressed in all black, she stood over Alzuhur with her steak knife in hand.

Ange peered down at her prey and said, (in Arabic): 'Do you remember me?' Alzuhur remained confused, so Ange waited. In time, she watched his face change.

The man's face transformed from confused to terrified in an instant. He tried to yell from under the tape gag.

'That's right! You son of a pig,' Ange growled. 'Tonight, you will die in the most horrible way. But first your wife will learn what you did to me in prison.'

Alzuhur squirmed against his confinements, making inaudible noises.

Ange took half a step back and kicked him three times in the stomach with her heavy boots. She aimed for his liver, but Alzuhur twisted at the last second and she burst his spleen. Alzuhur stopped moving and his eyes rolled back in shock.

Ange went to his wife.

Over the next few minutes, Ange told the woman what her husband had done to her in prison. She could see the woman slump as she heard the horrific account. The woman's eyes were now on Alzuhur.

She no longer looked concerned, or even afraid. Her look was a mix of pure disgust and loathing for the man she was long forced to endure.

Ange was ready to end it. Her plan was to make Alzuhur suffer before she killed him. It was a detailed menu of pain.

But as she moved toward her old tormenter, a strange wariness came over her. A deep emptiness, as though her long held pool of rage and hate was draining away.

By the time she reached Alzuhur, she realized the death-dealing element inside her soul had suddenly vanished.

She was done.

Like a wave of warm water, a deep desire for peace and quiet rolled over her. All she wanted, at this moment, was to return to Mack and the boys in Japan.

Was this the moment her father talked about? Was the lion inside her coming to rest? She looked down at Alzuhur and knew that killing him would also kill what remained of her humanity.

She shuddered, wrapping her arms around her chest. She felt a single tear rolled down her cheek.

Ange looked back at Alzuhur's wife and could see the woman was finished. She had taken her revenge and it was over.

She redressed into her shapeless smock and left the house.

After two separate flights, she was back in her Turkish apartment. Airport security in both Syrian and Turkey had no interest in this exhausted looking Turkish woman returning home.

The White House — Washington DC

CIA Director Arron Gearing requested Terrance Wolf to join him for a meeting with the President's national security team.

As they entered the meeting room, Wolf recognized Rosie Yen, the National Security Advisor and Chief of Staff Rolf Haines. But what surprised him was the presence of Lon Ripple, of Leaf Petroleum, Shane Coupling, the head of Natural Gases America, and Don Theck of Southern United Coal.

'Welcome, gentlemen,' said Chief of Staff Haines. 'Please, take a seat.'

As everyone sat around a large ornate table, White House staff arrived with trays of coffee and baked treats, placing them on the table.

'Help yourselves to coffee and food,' Haines told them with a warm smile. 'I'm sure you know everyone here.'

The CIA men nodded at the assembled group.

'As you know,' Haines continued, 'it's the policy of this White House to control the development of this, what do you call it?'

'We're just calling it the "Free Energy Project",
Director Gearing told him.

'Okay, fine. The Free Energy Project,' Haines said.

'You see,' NSA Yen began, 'we believe that the
proliferation of this technology, on an international scale,
could become the single greatest threat to global stability.'

'That's correct,' Haines joined in. 'The men in this
room employ directly, and indirectly, over ten million
Americans. Times that by five globally. The capital stake
they have in our economy is massive. Then there are the
related downstream industries; mining and drilling
equipment, the auto industry, gas retailers, and the list goes
on.'

'You see boys?' Don Theck (Southern United Coal)
started speaking. 'We are not just producing energy. We
support entire economies. What do you think would
happen if millions of people were laid off because some
smartass scientist builds a box with an antenna that lets
you suck free electricity out of the sky?'

Arron Gearing and Terrance Wolf sat impassively
through the show. They knew what was happening. These
men were the President's most prolific financial backers,
and they were scared.

For generations men like these had kept clean energy
technology at bay. They lobbied and won for unregulated
emissions and the suppression of electric cars. They fought
against solar and wind projects, pouring hundreds of
millions of dollars into super PACs to help elect one
corrupt President after another.

All to one end; to keep America and the world burning fossil fuels and to make these men money. Vast sums of unregulated, mostly tax-free money.

'Now tell us,' Haines asked. 'Where are you in catching our, what did you call them, the three little bears?'

'Yes, sir,' Gearing said. 'We have tracked them to La Paz, Mexico after they evaded our surveillance team in California. It appears they have help from a foreign government, or well-resourced unknown entities. We believe they have escaped to somewhere in the Americas to hole up and continue their project.'

'The Americas! Goddammit!' Haines exclaimed. 'What's the next step?'

'I'll let Wolf fill you in on our progress,' Gearing told him.

'We have set up a command post in La Paz and will remain there until we have exhausted all possible leads,' Wolf began. 'I have compiled a list of likely governments who may be harbouring our fugitives. I have brought in the State Department to help in this. We will be cross-checking flight arrivals against departure times at all major points south. Frankly, this search is a needle in a haystack. Based on our target's previous behaviour, they could employ any number of evasion techniques and could be holed up in one of dozens of cities.'

Director Gearing could see Haines was becoming frustrated. Haines needed something concrete to take back to the President.

'Sir,' Gearing jumped in. 'You can tell the President our investigation hinges on tracing a flight from either La Paz, Carbo, or Tijuana on the Baja Sur. We are confident they did not drive back into the US. We have thrown a net over the border just in case.'

'Thrown a fucking net?' Haines had lost his southern charm. 'It seems your nets don't hold these assholes!'

'Yes, sir,' Gearing persisted. 'However, once we trace the plane, we can locate the targets. We have a Langley Red Team of analysts working on their possible next steps. This team employs behavioural experts and use computer modelling.'

'Behaviour experts and computer games! What's next? A Ouija Board?' Haines asked. 'There were too many what-ifs in your report, gentlemen. But it is what it is. Just find these guys as fast as you can before the President gets involved personally. The man is a complete fucking moron, and nobody wants that, trust me.'

The meeting was over and the CIA men were dismissed. The President's energy flunkies remained.

Don Theck (Southern United Coal) heaved himself to his feet. 'Get the President in here.'

'You're speaking directly to the President when you speak to me,' Haines reminded him. 'You know our clown of a President has not survived this long with the trail of shit he has left behind him without always using firewall. I am his fucking firewall.'

'Okay! Okay, then listen up,' Theck said firmly. 'We want this free energy bullshit stamped out permanently.

We want the players removed, and all their fucking research documents destroyed.'

Lon Ripple (Leaf Petroleum) joined the fray. 'We financed this lump of shit President knowing the man is a complete fuckup and mob criminal. So let me make this clear; if you do not fix this, our money is gone. Our political support is gone, and you will be left swinging in the breeze. Is that clear enough for you?'

Haines hated his job. *How the hell did he get stuck with this President?* He asked himself once again.

Gearing and Wolf were escorted out of the meeting, and made their way to the visitors' car park where they paused for a moment on the path.

'My God, I wished I still smoked,' Gearing told Wolf. 'Who have you got on the ground down there?'

'Rene Zeist,' Wolf told him.

'I know that name. Wasn't she the one who caught the cell of Saudis funding ISIS a few years back? How's her fast-moving target work? Can she get down in the mud?'

'She came up through law enforcement, and the DEA,' Wolf told him. 'She killed two high value targets in Columbo, taking a round in the chest. She also has a healthy string of other kills.'

'There's no point in sending you down there,' Gearing told him. 'Liaise with Zeist on the phone. I may need you in Washington in case we're called back to the White House. Just remember, if we go before the President, no big words and use short sentences.

Wolf nodded. 'Copy that.'

La Paz, Mexico

CIA Field Agent in Charge Rene Zeist was operating from her command post onboard the purpose-built C-130.

Zeist had scanned the La Paz roadway and airport security camera footage several times. She watched her fugitives hire a car and drive toward the city of La Paz. They covered their faces well and used fake IDs. *Nothing to help her there*, she thought and sighed.

It took some doing, but she retrieved the in-car GPS code and downloaded the trip details.

'Cabo San Lucas!' she called to her team. 'The car is in Cabo!' They stopped working and joined her by the consol.

'Aeroporto de Cabo San Lucas International to be exact!' She told them. 'Get me all the camera footage of the airport and a list of planes that departed that day.'

Three hours later, Zeist had footage of her five fugitives going through the airport and boarding a Gulfstream G550.

'Okay! I have you, now where are you going in such a big plane?' she asked the empty air.

Enduring eight diplomatic phone calls and with the application of much pressure, Zeist got her answer.

'They flew to Chile,' Zeist reported to Wolf.

'Do you know who chartered the plane?' Wolf asked.

'I'm working on it, sir,' Zeist told him. 'I'm getting a lot of pushback from the Chilean authorities. You may need to call state again.'

'US-Chilean relations are crap right now over that oil deal,' Wolf told her. 'Are you up for a little field work, Rene? Get down there and bust heads if you need to, just be discreet.'

'Copy, sir,' she said. 'I'll be down there tonight.'

'Take a small team. You and two guys, and don't get arrested,' Wolf told her. 'I can't come down there to bail you out; I was involved in a thing a few years back, and well, let's say I'm not their favourite American.'

'Copy that,' she said. She had heard a story about a ranking CIA agent who came to Chile to rescue an American family in a kidnapping a few years back. Legend has it some people died, including the son of a politician who was the kidnapping gang leader.

Zeist thought it sounded all urban legend, but maybe it was Wolf.

'We're balls deep in this now, Rene. You can stop calling me sir. Terry is fine,' he told her.

'Yes, sir.'

Wolf chuckled and hung up.

Osaka, Japan

Angelina Cohen put her travel documents away and looked up to see Mack waiting for her at the arrival gate.

He could see she was exhausted with a jumper tied around her shoulders and trailing her luggage. Her typical long stride power walk had been replaced by a casual stroll.

Mack could also see she was not wearing makeup and her hair was a mess. He surmised something had knocked the wind out of her.

'Hey, girl,' he said simply.

Without saying a word, she grabbed him up into a bear hug, folding her body into his.

'It's good to be home,' she whispered in his ear.

The pair stood there embraced at the arrivals gate for long time.

'Let's get you out of here,' Mack eventually said and kissed her on the cheek.

'I'll run you a bath and get some proper food.'

The pair walked out of the airport without speaking and entered a white lab van.

Time away from Ange was always hard for Mack. For him, Ange was part of his life-energy. When she was gone, he felt lost and empty.

As the van pulled into airport traffic, Ange rested her head on his shoulder. With his free hand, he stroked her hair in mutual pleasure. The very touch of her, even after all these years, gave him a buzz that nothing on this earth could compare.

'It's good to be home,' she whispered again. 'Home is where you are.'

Ange was not naturally effusive, but when she chose to say something romantic, her words were powerful. What she said filled Mack with unsurpassed joy.

Back at the lab, Ange took a long bath and ate. The food was all traditional Japanese, with lots of fish, pickles, rice, and assorted vegetables.

She then went to her room to sleep, reappearing three hours later looking happy and relaxed.

Lucas, John, and Kurt dropped their work and raced to greet her. There was much hugging and small talk about this and that. She felt a warmth for them she had never felt for anyone, outside of her own father.

Ange asked about Sam Kimura; learning she was in Tokyo rustling up money from the government.

'Let me catch you up!' Mack told her enthusiastically.

Ange let Mack talk about gadgets and algorithms until he wore himself out. This project was his lifelong dream, and he was so close to realising it.

At any other time in her life, Ange would have been bored to death and looking for an exit. But not today. She felt a deep contentment listening to him talk and the sound of his voice. She felt like she had a family of her own.

The team ate dinner together and Ange got to know some of the Japanese engineers. They were very quiet and excessively polite.

By nine p.m., Sam had returned. She gave Ange a big hug and they all enjoyed celebratory drinks. Sam wanted to hear about her father and what they got up to.

Sam then gave everyone the news of another thirty-million-dollar investment.

More drinks followed. It was a happy time for all.

Later that night Mack took Ange by the hand and put his mouth on her neck, but she gently held him back.

'Not tonight,' she told him in a small voice. 'I need some time.' Mack didn't quite understand, but he respected her needs.

'Take all the time you need,' he told her. 'I'm here when you want to talk.'

'I know. I love you.'

Arturo Merino Benítez Airport. Santiago, Chile

Rene Zeist and her team of two specialists landed in the capital just before midnight. It was a long wait getting a flight from La Paz, as this was not a common destination from that part of Mexico.

She used her time well. Her team had hacked the charter details of all the private jet hire companies who flew large Gulfstreams. And only one leased the intercontinental G550 matching her target's colour scheme. Zeist now had the name and home address of the company director.

From the airport, Zeist and her team hired a plain white van and drove an indirect route to the local CIA safe house. They circled the block twice to clear the route. There were many foreign governments who'd like to know where the CIA safe houses are located.

The house was in an average looking suburb and surrounded by trees on all sides. The team drove up the driveway and disappeared.

The house manager called himself Jeff and was a junior field operative.

It could be a long tedious tour of duty, but all the "Jeffs" had to endure it as part of their fieldwork probation.

So far, Jeff had done good work. The house was well prepared with all the weapons, equipment, and the technology Rene Zeist had ordered.

Beyond that it was pure need to know. Jeff asked no questions and was given no information.

When the team had finished checking the equipment, they had a chance to eat a decent meal and sleep.

'Good grub, Jeff!' Zeist told him.

'I don't get many visitors, so I thought I'd go all out for you,' he told her.

'Just remember, we're not officially here either,' she remined him.

The young agent nodded.

Early the next morning Zeist and her team drove to the address of the home of one Matias Benitez. The team positioned the van for the best camera view and waited.

Experience taught the team not to drink coffee, or to eat, as bathroom breaks would not be on their horizon for some time.

At eight a.m., there was movement at the house. The garage door rolled up and the family minibus backed out, driven by, who they assumed was, Mrs Benitez. She strapped in and called for her children.

'Start filming,' Zeist said.

As the camera operated, three children ran out of the house pushing and shoving each other playing their morning games. Mrs Benitez chided them and herded them into the minibus. They reversed down the driveway and headed toward the local school with the CIA van trailing.

At the school, Zeist's cameraman got ample footage of the children entering the school. They talked and laughed with their friends while the camera rolled.

'Got enough?' she asked.

The agent nodded.

'Back to the house,' she said.

The CIA van did a U-turn and drove with cautious speed back to the Benitez home. They parked in the driveway and entered the house through the unlocked front door.

Matias Benitez was seated at the breakfast table, and before he could speak a stream of taser prongs pierced his chest followed by fifty thousand volts of electricity.

The CIA operatives placed a hood over his head and carried him out of the house. They heaved him into the van and drove away.

'Heavy fucker,' an agent grunted.

'Burrito munching motherfucker, and I think he shat himself,' the second agent commented.

'Enough!' Zeist snapped. 'Watch your speed.'

She checked her watch. 'One minute, ten seconds. Not too bad boys. Maybe a company record.'

When Benitez came around, he found himself strapped tightly to a chair. He strained and twisted against his confinements until a voice from the shadows shouted, 'Alto!'

Benitez stopped instantly.

The room was dark, except for the light from a flatscreen TV ten feet away. Next to the TV was a large CIA operative dressed in non-American issue tactical gear holding a submachine gun.

Benitez started yelling, but the CIA man raised his finger to his mouth in the silence gesture.

Benitez fell silent.

Zeist stood behind him.

'Mr Benitez, can you hear me?' Zeist asked in Spanish.

His twisted his head to identify the speaker but failed.

'I can hear you. If this is a kidnapping, you must know I have no cash. All my money is in the business,' he replied.

'This is not a kidnapping,' Zeist told him. 'In fact, it's much simpler than that. All I want is some information, then you are free to go home unharmed. Do you understand what I said?'

'Si,' he acknowledged her. 'But I am a simple businessman, there is nothing...' Zeist pressed play on her device and the screen came to life with images of Benitez's children leaving the house and playing at the school.

Benitez let out a moan. He understood the gravity of his situation.

'Tell me what you want,' he said, knowing he was defeated. 'I will tell you.'

Two hours later, Benitez woke up on a bus station bench with a group of nuns looking down at him shaking their heads.

Zeist and her team had already returned to the airport, where they chartered a light plane flight south to Maquehue Airport, Temuco.

Benitez had given her the name of an organisation that hired the Gulfstream, called Le Frontier de Science. It was headed by a man called Manuel Alvarez who was based on Isla Mocha.

From Temuco, they chartered a helicopter and flew to Mocha. It was still only 4pm when they arrived and visibility was excellent.

'Here is Mocha,' the pilot declared. 'Can you tell me what you're looking for?'

'Just do a circuit for me, por favor,' Zeist asked him.

Within minutes she spotted it.

'What's that, in the centre of the island?' she asked.

'Oh, that is a very hush-hush new research centre. The government people won't let us fly anywhere near that.'

Zeist went into her carry bag and brought out a wad of US dollars.

'Will this get us closer?' she asked.

The pilot looked at the money and ran his hand through his hair.

'Ci, Señora,' he told her.

The chopper began a descending circuit of the complex.

'Not too close,' she warned.

The pilot extended his range and continued the circuit. Zeist could see vehicles and smoke coming from chimneys. People were moving about, but they didn't look like western scientists or construction workers. They appeared to be local villagers.

Zeist could see vehicles, but once again they were old bangers. These were not the vehicles used by wealthy Americans. Something was very wrong with this scene.

'Put us down in that flat area,' she told him.

'I could lose my license,' the pilot complained.

Zeist brought out more money, and the pilot commenced his landing.

On the ground, Zeist could see there were no Americans here. The locals had taken over the place. She spoke to one old woman who told her it was the strangest thing; for months construction teams worked on the buildings and one day they all left. They left and nobody came back.

Zeist was shocked. She ruffled back her hair and asked, 'How long ago did they leave?'

The woman told her it was about one month ago.

The woman asked Zeist if it was all right if the people used the buildings.

'Sure, knock yourselves out.'

Zeist and her team searched all the buildings and found nothing of interest. Each building was empty of anything that resembled lab material or equipment. It appeared to Zeist the complex was never intended for use.

The team also searched for trash but were told all the trash was burned. There was no trace of her scientists or anything else.

'I think we've been duped,' she said to herself. 'Anyone got ideas?'

Her two operatives suggested integrating a few of the locals and staking out the place for a few days.

'I am under strict instructions not to leave a footprint down here,' she told them. 'I'm pretty sure the apprehension and terrorising of local farmers would be noticed. Besides, why would our targets tell the locals anything?'

The CIA team stood for a while watching the lab and considering their options.

'Whatever happened here, we missed it,' Rene Zeist declared. 'A stakeout won't help us now. We're heading back to Temuco, but first I have to phone Wolf.'

As the team made their way back to the chopper, they saw a local man talking to the pilot.

'This looks interesting,' Zeist told her team as they approached the chopper.

'This man just asked where the Americans have gone,' the pilot told Zeist. 'He says the construction people hired him to do some labour.'

'They went back to America,' Zeist said (in Spanish). 'Did you know them well?'

'Si,' the man said. 'I worked here for many days. They paid me in cash, and I want to know if they need me for more work.'

Rene Zeist viewed the man. She knew at once this could be their first real lead in the case.

'I have been told they might be back next month,' she lied. 'What is your name? I can tell them you are looking for work.'

'Oh, that would be very good, Señora,' the man smiled broadly. 'My name is Manual Harada and I am a carpenter and roof builder.'

'Thank you, Manual,' Zeist told him. 'You know, I heard they are going to build another building. I'm sure they'll need a carpenter for that. Who was the American boss man here?'

'His name is Señor Jeff,' Manual said. 'Jeff Tyndall.' Zeist nodded to the CIA men and smiled.

'Can you wait here for a moment?' she asked Manual. 'I'll phone Jeff now and see if he has work for you.'

Manual was very excited at the prospect of making more money and nodded many times.

Zeist went back to the chopper and pulled out her tablet. She began a search for a Jeffery Tyndall, tagging construction and building. Four profiles were returned, taking all of thirty seconds.

She returned to Manual and showed him the selection of images representing all the Jeff Tyndalls.

Manual recognized him at once and pointed to the man he knew.

'Si, Si! This is Señor Jeff!'

Rene Zeist made a show of attempting a fake call to Señor Jeff.

'I'm sorry Manual, I can't get through. I'll call him again later for you.'

The team flew back to Temuco and caught a regional flight back to Santiago. Before they landed, Zeist had Jeffery Michael Tyndall's full bio. She had his tax records, banking, cellular phone, and internet history.

'He's in Vegas,' Zeist reported to Wolf. 'His credit card was swiped at the Bellagio two days ago,' she announced.

'I'll put a local team on him,' Wolf told her. 'You get back to La Paz and fly the C-130 to Nellis Air Force Base. I'll have Tyndall on ice waiting for you.'

Zeist wanted to be part of the arrest but knew the time lag in her getting back to Las Vegas would be too long.

Upon arrival at Santiago, Zeist discovered there were no flights to La Paz, so she chartered a jet. She had hardly slept in thirty-six hours and a desperate fatigue seeped into her bones. She covered her face with a jacket and slept for the entire flight.

Late that night the team landed at La Paz. The crew had fully prepped the C-130 and were ready for take-off, for a scheduled arrival at Nellis by three a.m.

Too pumped to sleep in flight, Zeist searched the Cabo San Lucas airport security videos again.

She had found some obscure footage from a hanger camera that pointed toward the apron where her target Gulfstream sat.

Using video enhancement software, she cleaned up the images and focused in on the plane. She watched closely as each of her targets boarded the plane.

What she saw next rocked her back in her seat.

'Japanese,' she whispered. 'The people waiting inside the jet were all Japanese.'

Nellis Airforce Base

Zeist and her team flashed their IDs at the base security guards and were led to a waiting jeep. Minutes later they had entered an old hangar next to a disused runway.

In the centre of the hangar, she viewed a large, heavyset man handcuffed to a chair. A spotlight was directly in front of him, flooding the man in bright white light.

Three armed agents were positioned around the man.

To Zeist's surprise, Wolf himself was there. He made his way over to her.

'Do you want to do this?' he asked.

Zeist nodded and went to the cuffed man. She stood behind and to the left of the light.

'Jeffery Tyndall?' Zeist asked.

Tyndall raised his head. He looked like death warmed up.

'Mr Tyndall, you built a research facility on the island of Mocha, Chile. Is that correct?' Zeist asked, slowly and clearly.

'What? Yes, Mocha. We built a lab,' Tyndall said, now very confused. 'What the fuck is all this?'

'Mr Tyndall.' Zeist maintained a calm tone. 'You are not under suspicion here, but you are being held under the

Federal Espionage Act of 2003. We are simply looking for the man who commissioned the lab.'

Tyndall had worked with Mackenzie James for over ten years as a construction manager. Some of that work was done in secrecy to avoid the attention of unwanted parties. Yet he could never have imagined his own government would ever arrest him.

This was America, Tyndall told himself. As such, he had the right to silence until he spoke to a lawyer.

He then looked around the room at the silhouetted armed guards. He saw they wore no uniforms or FBI windbreakers. His instincts told him this situation was extremely unorthodox.

'Who exactly are you people?' he asked.

'We are federal government agents,' Zeist told him. 'The man who commissioned the building project on Mocha has committed serious crimes against the United States and we need your help to find him.'

'I know my rights,' Tyndall told her confidently. 'I wish to speak to my lawyer.'

'A lawyer can't help you here, Mr Tyndall.' Zeist bored in. 'We are not going to charge you with a crime. You are a party to espionage. As such, you are beyond the protection of the law.'

'What the fuck does that mean?' Tyndall was mustering his bravado, but fear was beginning to grip him.

'We have a jet right outside on the apron ready to fly you to a CIA black site,' Zeist began. 'There you will be integrated for as long as we need to. Typically, this process takes days, but the strong ones can last a week or more.'

She gave him time to process this scenario.

'Are you a strong one, Mr Tyndall?' Zeist asked. 'Will you last a week with us?'

Jeff Tyndall suddenly felt ill as the reality of the moment struck him.

'We know your boss is hiding Japan. We also know you have no further role in this charade.'

Zeist took up a position directly in front of him and bent down to his level. 'You are simply a pawn in this elaborate charade. Therefore, we do not want you. We want your boss. Do you understand me?'

Tyndall considered his options.

'Tell the name of the person you built the lab for,' she said softly. 'Tell me and you will be driven back to your hotel.'

Tyndall nodded and Rene Zeist stood up.

'Fuck with me, Jeff,' she began. 'Give me just one piece of false information. Lie to me in any way, and these men with guns will spend the next week extracting the information from you. Nod if you understand that?'

Tyndall looked up at the agents and nodded.

'Who do work for?' she asked.

Tyndall grunted something inaudible.

Zeist nodded to the guards who moved in and removed Tyndall's shackles.

'Help Mr Tyndall over to the table,' Zeist told the guards. 'He needs some water and coffee. Do it now!'

Ten minutes later Zeist found Wolf.

'Mackenzie James, the American green energy billionaire,' she told him. 'It figures. He's been all over the world building energy sites. Tyndall was just a pawn in this and doesn't know anything else. What do you think about the Japanese on the Gulfstream?'

Wolf could see Zeist was exhausted, but he liked her Japan link theory.

'I want Tyndall polygraphed,' Wolf told her.

'I'll order it now,' Zeist confirmed. 'Then can I cut him loose?'

'Bug his car and hotel room and get a tracker on his jacket before you let him go,' Wolf instructed. 'I won't start trusting this guy until this thing is over.'

Wolf looked at his agent. Rene Zeist was a naturally good-looking lady. Thirty-five, red hair, and pretty face. But right now, she looked exhausted.

'Rene, I want you to take twenty-four hours off. You're no good to me half dead. Get a nice hotel room here in Vegas. Eat, get a massage, and sleep. The day after tomorrow, meet me at Langley for the next phase.'

Zeist considered protesting, then looked up to see sunshine beam in through a hanger window. It was then she realized she was done.

'Copy that,' she told Wolf in a small voice. Wolf chuckled.

'Been quite a ride, hey?' he mused.

Rene Zeist laughed too. But her laugh was not a healthy sound. To Wolf, it sounded more like an unspooling jet engine.

Wolf walked her to a military jeep and watched his agent drive off into the desert dawn.

'You sure know how to pick 'em, old boy,' Wolf told himself.

CIA Head Office Langley, Virginia

Operations Centre "A" housed a team of three analysts seated at a long table with audio visual technicians at either end. The technicians operated the drones, satellites, and ground-asset communications.

On the front wall was a huge screen with smaller screens running down either side of it.

Rene Zeist had been in this room a few times, yet it never failed to impress. From here, the CIA can spy on anyone or anything on the globe. The combined assets can track and observe multiple targets via drones or satellites with ground radars, high-definition optics, thermal or laser wall penetrating cameras, right down to human assets on the ground.

From this room, Rene Zeist could fire a hellfire missile, from a predator drone, into the window of any home, building, or vehicle the CIA deemed a threat to the United States. If need be, she could drop a two-thousand-pound bomb on a terrorist training camp from a carrier-based F18 flying at fifty thousand feet.

'You look better,' Wolf told her.

Zeist did as she was ordered. She had taken a break and was now partially refreshed. She was ready for business.

'Yes, sir. Now let's find these bastards.'

'There were hundreds of potential airports and thousands of flights landing across the Japanese archipelago every day,' Wolf told her. 'It's going to be one hell of job finding one private plane.'

'Then we should get started,' Zeist told him.

The hours of searching became days. Then a week passed by, as the men and women in Operations Centre A slaved at the awesome task of looking for a needle in a haystack.

Typically, the satellite imagery databank was erased after a week, as the data storage volume was so vast. Zeist ordered all erasing to cease for Japan and Korea in the time periods of the flight.

As time rolled by, Wolf could see Zeist was working eighteen-hour days and was, once again, completely exhausted.

'You are out of here right now!' Wolf ordered. 'Hit the gym, have a meal, and sleep for eight hours. Security will arrest you if you try to re-enter this room for twelve hours.'

Wolf started the timer on his watch.

'Ah, I don't think so, Sir,' Zeist protested. 'We're getting close, I can feel it.'

'All you can feel is goal fever, which means you're not thinking straight,' Wolf corrected her. 'By my count, you're only half-done. Prepare yourself for the fact they landed on a strip with poor satellite coverage, or they flew to Korea. Knowing our three little bears, that's entirely possible.'

She began to complain but he held up a large blunt finger and waved it at her.

Rene Zeist finally relented and exited the operations room. She found the CIA gym and went to work hard on the machines and boxing bag.

With every lift repetition, push-up, and bag punch, Zeist ran though the details of her operation, searching for flaws in her process. She examined her methods and performed a "what-if" analysis. Finally, she was satisfied she had done it right.

The next day she returned to work renewed and clearheaded, seeing the room was alive with activity.

They found something! she told herself.

Zeist found Wolf in the centre of the room watching images on the main display screen.

'You're looking at a disused Japanese airbase north of Osaka,' Wolf told her. 'We would have found it sooner, but the Japanese banned us taking high-definition images of their military bases. We cleaned up these images.'

Zeist knew at once that she was looking at the image of her Gulfstream. The jet was the same make and model as her target plane.

'This would be one hell of a coincidence if it wasn't our guys,' Zeist told him.

'The site is registered as an unused air base,' Wolf continued. 'Yet, look at all the security. Armed guards at the gates and vehicle barriers. They even have roaming patrols throughout the complex.'

'We need to get a look inside those buildings,' Zeist told him. 'Can we run a drone in?'

'The air force has just finished trials on the Grumman X-47A stealth drone at Mable Base,' Wolf told her. 'They're fitting it with spy lasers for us right now.'

Rene Zeist knew the X-47A specs. It can loiter over a target for up to 24 hours and is invisible to ground radars.

Thirty minutes later, a technician announced drone footage was coming in. The high-definition images gave a crystal-clear view of the target site, and Langley was handed drone control.

'Start with the smaller buildings, then work your way up,' Wolf told the pilot.

The team watched silently as the drone completed its search. The images were so clear and close it was like being there.

'There!' Zeist called. 'What's that, off to the left?'

'Reposition to the northwest quadrant,' Wolf ordered.

The drone repositioned and as the images came in, they could see people moving about near a clump of square buildings.

'We need to see inside that larger building,' Zeist said.

'Switch to laser and scan it,' Wolf instructed the camera operator.

Two seconds later, a new image appeared on screen. The drone-mounted laser penetrated walls and the roof, returning a green-screen digital interpretation of the building internals.

'Looks like an engineering lab to me,' Zeist told Wolf.

'We need a full evaluation before we get too excited. Get our tech analysist onto this. I want to know exactly what this equipment is, and what its used for,' Wolf advised.

'Go back to optical camera,' Wolf told the tech. 'I want as many facial images as we can get.'

As the camera scanned the scene, the image clearly showed two men standing outside the main target building. In one fateful moment, the first man looked up to the sky.

Rene Zeist gasped. 'Mackenzie James!' she whispered.

'If I'm not mistaken, the second man is—' Wolf began.

'Lucas Harding.' Zeist finished Wolf's statement for him. Wolf squeezed her shoulder.

'We've got 'em!' he told her.

The team silently watched the screen for a few more seconds. After one of the most tedious tracking operations in recent CIA history, they finally reached pay dirt.

'Okay, people, listen up!' Wolf told his team. 'Firstly, good work from all of you. Looks like you'll get to go home soon. Second, go grab a coffee and snacks. Be back at your posts in twenty minutes.'

Everyone clapped Wolf and themselves.

'Join me in the mess,' Wolf told Zeist.

Wolf and Zeist took a table away from the main group. Zeist drank some coffee but could taste nothing. All she wanted to do is go back to work.

'Relax now, and take a breath,' Wolf told her. 'I've spent most of my life working counterintelligence, and the number one lesson I learned is; never rush, take time to think, and evaluate every detail.'

Zeist took a deep breath and nodded.

'What now?' she asked. 'This is a highly tenuous situation. Japan is one our closest allies.'

'Correct. Which means our options are strictly limited. Apprehension and extraction are off the table, so we'll be exploring other options,' Wolf told her matter-of-factly.

Zeist knew immediately what that meant. This operation had just shifted from investigatory to military.

'Do I remain at my post?' she asked Wolf.

He considered her question for a moment, and knew things were about to get ugly. If Rene Zeist stayed, she would be blooded on a whole new level.

Is she ready for that? They were about to commit an international crime, and if things went badly, heads would roll. Perhaps all the way to Leavenworth prison.

'There is no requirement for you to remain at this post,' Wolf told her. 'Your job was to find them, and you did.'

Zeist watched his face, looking for clues as to what to do.

'However, if you choose to stay, it will expand your CIA resume,' Wolf told her. 'Just be careful what you wish for. Once you shift into the blood and bucket side of this business, you will be slotted. Do you understand?'

She understood. Her name will go on the list of agents called on for wet work assassinations. It surprised her, but she never considered herself a killer. She had needed to kill in her career, but it was always in self-defence, and in the line of duty. She had never been sent on a specific kill-mission.

'If you want to be part of the next stage of this mission, you have to say it,' Wolf told her.

'I understand what's coming, and I want to stay,' she said in a firm voice that betrayed her actual conviction.

Wolf searched her face for a few seconds, then nodded.

'Follow me,' he told her.

The pair walked down the corridor and entered a smaller conference room filled with military officers. They took the last two remaining seats.

Rene Zeist had a dozen sets of eyes on her. Her face flushed and she suddenly felt sick. It had been a long time since she felt out of her pond.

'Gentlemen,' Wolf began. 'What have you got for me?'

Over the next thirty minutes, Wolf and the military men discussed their actionable options. The goal was to interdict the target inside a technically advanced, friendly country, while leaving no evidence of US involvement.

'We have ruled out guided missiles, air-to-ground bombing, and precision drone strikes,' Wolf announced. 'All of these actions can be tracked by the Japanese military. A ground assault will be too messy and slow. Extraction would also be a nightmare.'

At the end of the discussion only one practical option presented itself.

'So be it,' Wolf announced. 'The world's most technologically advanced military is going use a two-hundred-year-old kill method.'

He slammed the table with his fist, closing the briefing.

The Japanese Lab

Mack knew that research scientists on the scent of a major breakthrough operate on a level mere mortals could never understand.

It had become his preoccupation just keeping his boys alive and functioning. He oversaw their food intake, sleep patterns, and mental health.

Yet, his efforts weren't enough as Lucas, John, and Kurt pushed themselves and their Japanese team through eighteen, and nineteen-hour days.

After six weeks of frantic effort, Mack could see cracks emerge. Mistakes and shortcuts started to appear and costly reworks, even the dumping of huge data packages had occurred.

'We are working on a method for release of cosmic energy,' Mack told Ange. 'Our team is now one hundred percent goal focused and I'm worried risk management is being neglected.'

'They're also snapping at each other and their teams,' Ange said confirming his concerns.

'We have to make some changes,' Mack said. 'This project is a marathon, not a sprint. I need you to build a stress management plan for them. We need to address their diet, exercise, and sleep. We also need an R&R plan.'

'I have just the thing,' Ange told him. 'They'll fight it, so you need to be tough on them.'

'First up,' Mack started, 'they need a break from this place right now. Get the bus ready.'

The team was assembled in the main meeting room. Mack stood and asked them to follow him.

'We are all going off-site,' he told them. 'You're all having a nice long breakfast break!'

'I can't go,' Lucas told him. 'A new resonance amplifier is coming in today. I must install a housing frame and check…'

'No, you don't,' Ange told him. 'You need to unplug for an hour before you touch that thing.'

Lucas attempted to stare down Ange. Discovering this was effort was futile, he blinked first and left the room, muttering something about fornication and a close relative.

'What did you say?' Ange asked.

'Nothing,' Lucas told her.

Haru Takahashi, the Japanese team leader, thought Mack was a soft touch. He knew Americans were an overindulged race, but didn't say anything.

On the way out the door, Ange grabbed Mack by the arm. 'I need a word with you about security,' she told him.

'Can it wait?' he asked.

'I'll be quick.'

'Okay, go.'

'Let me tell you something about the CIA from my years of first-hand experience,' Ange began. 'You can fool them once, maybe twice. You can even lead them down false trails, but here's the thing. You have made fools of them, and this is now personal. It means they won't stop until they find you.'

'Find us,' Mack corrected her.

'Don't fuck around with me on this,' Ange told him. 'This is my pond. I can rattle off a dozen techniques they will employ. If it were me, I'd find you.'

Mack knew she was right. But this was a bad time to uproot the whole operation and move. The setback would kill their progress.

'Okay, smart girl,' Mack said. 'What would you have me do?'

'You know what I think. Movement is the only way to stay ahead of these people. We have been here far too long.'

'We are in the final stages of this project,' Mack began. 'The boys are getting ready to build test beds. A move at this stage would cost us another two months at least. Besides, what can the CIA do to us here?'

'What can they do to us here?' Ange scoffed. 'Are you kidding me? The CIA has a long track record of hitting high-value targets wherever they choose,' Ange told him. 'They won't drop a bomb or invade the site. They will kill us remotely and leave no evidence.'

'Hang on just a minute! Japan is one of America's closest allies. They will not risk an international incident just to hit us!'

'I can't believe you are so fucking naive!' she scorned him. 'They have been killing people in allied countries for decades. Today, with all the technology at their disposal, killing is easy. Killing undetected is even easier.'

Mack instinctively knew she was right. But the cost in time and money to move was abhorrent to him.

'Let me think about it,' Mack told her. 'After breakfast I'll talk to Haru.'

Ange shrugged and headed back toward the lab.

'Are you coming?' he called after her.

'I don't eat breakfast, remember?' Ange told him, while Mack watched her walk away.

'Stubborn woman,' he muttered. But her words left him feeling disturbed and uncertain. A voice in his head reminded him about the dangers of false confidence hubris.

Every morning at seven am, a FedEx truck arrived at the front gate. It was checked and passed through into the complex to deliver lab parts and equipment.

On this day, the truck was intercepted four blocks from the air force base by four masked men in a black van. They levelled guns at the driver and forced him out of the cabin. The driver was bound and gagged, then thrown into the back of the van.

The FedEx truck was driven to a deserted sports field, followed by the CIA van.

Minutes later, the truck cargo was removed, and four heavy drums of refined ammonia nitrate mixed with diesel fuel were removed from the black van and loaded into the FedEx truck. A masked hijacker jumped in and armed the detonators.

The team replaced as much of the original cargo as possible to conceal the drums, and the truck continued along its route to the airbase.

The truck slowed to enter the old airbase access road, where it drove steadily toward the boom-gated security kiosk.

The guard was a Japanese army corporal coming to the end of this rotation. After a month of guard duty, he was bored from the lack of meaningful activity and eager to return to his training unit.

As he had done every morning, the guard strolled out to meet the truck and asked to see the paperwork. He had no idea what all the shipment particulars meant, but it was his job to tick them off the list.

'Open the back,' the guard instructed the driver.

The CIA driver was an American born man from a well to do Japanese immigrant family. He spoke the language fluently and was trained to act as a Japanese driver would.

The guard viewed dozens of small and large packages. He checked a few of the weights and cubic sizes on the consignment note. It looked the same as yesterday's shipment.

He sighed and signed the document.

'Show me your ID,' he ordered.

The driver took out his wallet and the guard examined his license against the man's face.

'Close it up and return to the truck,' he said automatically.

The guard watched the driver jump back into the cabin, then went to the security kiosk to call the lab and confirm the delivery. The guard scanned the license and consignment note. He walked back to the van and returned the documents to the driver.

'Do you know the way?' the guard asked.

'Straight down to the end and go right?'

The guard nodded and lifted the boom gate, waving him through.

CIA Operations Room Langley.

'The truck is through,' Zeist reported.

Their drone was back on station, providing crystal clear images of the proceedings.

As the Langley team watched, the truck slowly made its way deeper into the airbase.

A man Rene Zeist did not know walked up and handed Wolf a small black box with a keypad. Wolf typed in a code and a green light flashed on.

Above the keypad was a red trigger button.

The drone remained focused on the van as it made its last turn toward the lab. It reached its destination and stopped. The CIA team watched the driver get out and casually walk away.

'Pull the camera back fifteen percent,' Wolf instructed.

The camera angle widened, and the Langley team got a full view of the lab. They could see a man exit the lab, passing by the FedEx truck by just a few feet.

'Who the fuck is that?' Wolf asked.

'Oh shit! It's Mackenzie James,' Zeist almost yelled. He was their prime target, and right on cue he was walking directly past their bomb truck.

Without hesitation, Wolf pushed the detonation button, and the screen went white.

The explosion was so vast, the shockwave hit the drone some five thousand feet in the air. It tumbled several times before flight control could be re-established.

'Get the camera back on the target!' Wolf yelled.

As the smoke began to shift, the Langley team could see the blast damage.

All that was left was a smouldering heap. The lab was mostly gone, with its roof completely blown off. They could see fires burning inside the building and a heaped mass of broken machines.

'Go to thermal,' Wolf ordered.

The carnage was complete. Bodies and body parts were strewn everywhere. No one was moving.

'RTB the drone and bring up the satellite,' Wolf told the operator.

They watched the aftermath for a few more minutes, but there was very little to see. They had done their jobs, and nothing was left.

'Excuse me, please.' Zeist brushed past Wolf and made her way to the nearest toilet.

She made it just in time to be violently sick.

The scale of the violence and destruction had caught her by surprise. She thought she was mentally prepared for the interdiction, but the realisation she had just killed some thirty to forty people in a fraction of a second tripped her brain.

She threw up again and collapsed to the floor.

'What the fuck have I done?' she thought to herself.

The Aftermath

When the bomb exploded, Ange was in the conference room at the back of the lab. She was separated from the main building by three walls. When the blast hit, the shockwave blew her entire office's prefabricated section away from the main building, carrying her with it.

The young scientists were waiting in the bus parked in a concrete reinforced hanger. They were waiting for Mack, happy and hungry, looking forward to their break away to where a nice breakfast awaited them.

The shockwave hit the hanger like a wrecking ball. It blew the bus off its wheels and onto its side. Half of the hanger roof crumbled, dropping debris onto the upturned bus.

Several hours later, Angelina Cohen slowly opened her eyes and saw she was in a stark white cube. She wasn't very religious but knew at once this was heaven. Or, at least, heaven's waiting room.

Then a masked nurse appeared. Ange followed her to see she was adjusting a drip bottle hanging from a stainless-steel stand. She followed the drip lines and saw they went into her arm.

The shock of this sight was more than she could cope with, so she passed out.

When she awoke for the second time, Ange could feel pain.

'*Pain means I must be alive*,' she told herself.

She tried to identify its origin until she discovered the pain was everywhere.

'What… what, is happening?' Ange croaked. Her throat felt like sandpaper.

The nurse appeared again and took a long look at her. She then called for a doctor.

Ange blinked and saw a blurry man with a stethoscope standing beside her. The man was speaking, but Ange struggled to make sense of his words.

'Can you hear me? I am Doctor Inoue. Can you tell me your name please?'

Ange wondered about that for several seconds. *My name? What is my name?* Finally, a word came to her.

'Angelina,' she said. 'Can I have some water please?'

Doctor Inoue nodded to the nurse and a drinking tube was placed on her mouth.

'Very good, Angelina,' Inoue was speaking again. 'You are in a hospital. You, ah, had an accident.'

Ange looked around, now more confused than ever.

'An accident?' Ange asked. 'But how?'

'You need to sleep now,' Inoue told her.

His words worked like a drug, and Ange slept for another twelve hours.

Sam Kimura made her way to the hospital as soon as she heard the news. She arrived while Ange was still unconscious, but then found the boys. The hospital had placed them all in one ward protected by an armed security team.

Because they were in the bus, inside a hanger, Lucas, John and Kurt all survived the blast, suffering just a few cuts and scratches.

'How are Ange and Mack?' Lucas asked nervously. He knew they were not in a bunker.

Sam took a breath.

She realized no one had told them yet. She knew there was no easy way to say it, and the boys could see tears in her eyes.

'Ange is fine,' Sam began. 'She is sleeping, and the doctors are confident she'll make a full recovery. But, um, Mack is dead.'

The boys froze in place and stopped breathing. The words "Mack is dead" played over and over.

'No! No!' Kurt began yelling. 'I don't believe you! He could have escaped! Have you checked everywhere?'

Lucas jumped off his bed.

'That's right! He could have escaped. Come on, guys! Let's go find him!'

Sam knew she had lost control of the situation. She mustered all her strength to block the door.

'Boys, stop!' she forced the words out. 'We have his body. Mack is confirmed dead.'

They were stopped in their tracks. Tears welled in their eyes, while Sam let her own tears roll down her face uninterrupted.

Lucas grabbed Sam and held her tight. His crushing embrace comforted her and she went limp.

'How could they kill Mack?' he whispered in her ear.

He took Sam's face in his hands and looked into her eyes.

'How could they kill him?' he asked again. Sam's face was awash with tears.

'I don't know,' Sam sobbed. 'I just don't know.'

Two days later, Angelina Cohen had her medical consultation.

'You are recovering from a concussion and some hearing loss,' Doctor Inoue announced. 'It will return to normal over the next few days. You have fractures in your left cheek, left wrist, and four of your ribs. Your right arm and left leg are badly bruised. All of these will heal normally.'

Inoue flipped the chart to the next page.

'I have written you a recovery plan and assigned a physiotherapist. The concussion has affected your balance, so I suggest while moving around you use the wheelchair. If you take a fall, it will complicate your recovery. Do you want anything for the pain?'

'No doctor,' Ange told him. She wanted to feel all the pain. It was the physical pain that gave her the strength to go on. 'Thank you for treating me.'

'We have people you can talk to,' Inoue continued. 'Can I have a counsellor come by?'

Ange just stared at him, and he nodded. He got his answer and left the room. She felt like a lead veil had been dropped over her, trapping her in a dark empty place.

The violence and destruction of the bomb had taken her soulmate from her. Yet, she thanked God her boys survived.

Sam Kimura came to her room and was startled at what she saw.

Ange was propped up on her bed with her legs supported by pillows. Her exposed arms and legs were a mass of green and purple bruising.

Sam looked at her face. Her eyes were black, and her face was swollen to twice its normal size.

'You look like shit!' Sam told her.

Without realising it, this was exactly what Ange needed to hear. She spluttered out a scoff.

'Fuck you, bitch!' Sam laughed.

The two women just looked at each other, sharing time in their mutual loss and despair.

'The doctor said you're going to live,' Sam said. 'How long are you going to lay about for?'

Ange tried to move but the pain kept her in place. She wanted to punch Sam, but realized that in her condition, it would have to wait.

I'm sorry.' Sam smirked. 'I have a terrible bedside manner.'

'That's okay. I'll get you back when I can walk again.'

'As you know, the boys are fine and have left the hospital,' Sam told her. 'There will be a formal hearing into the bombing at the Ministry of Defence in Tokyo in two weeks. After the investigators have collected all the evidence.'

'The bomb was huge,' Ange said. 'There won't be much evidence.'

'It seems they hijacked a delivery truck and got through the front gate,' Sam reported. 'The residue shows ammonia nitrate. It's the same grade as commercial farm fertilizer.'

'Of course, it is.' Ange was far from surprised.

'Early estimates say some four hundred pounds of it exploded right next to the lab,' Sam continued. 'We didn't stand a chance.'

Ange had a startling recollection. 'Oh fuck, Sam! I held Mack back!'

'What?'

'Mack was taking the boys to breakfast,' Ange told her. 'I held him back for a meeting! He should have been in the bus with the boys. He should have been in the bunker when the bomb went off!'

Sam was silent.

'I killed Mack,' Ange said in a hollow voice.

'You did not! Ange, listen to me! You had no idea when they were going to trigger the bomb. They could have waited until the bus emerged from the bunker and killed all of them.'

But Sam could see that Ange had already shut down.

197

'Do you want some water?' Sam asked.

Ange did not answer. She lay motionless, staring at the ceiling.

'I'll come back later today,' Sam told her.

Post-recovery in Japan, Ange flew back to Israel and her father. Once again, Alatan Cohen was there to greet her at the airport.

Alatan could see his little girl looked older and her face had lost much of its animation. She had developed the thousand-yard stare of a war veteran. It was the look of a person always on guard.

Living in her family home, Ange went from wanting days of isolation to an unstoppable urge to drink and destroy herself. This oscillation between depressed solitude and mania endured for several weeks, until it finally reached a bloody climax.

In a soldiers' bar near the local base, she drank and slept with a few of the young soldiers. Tensions rose amongst some the men until the inevitable jealousy conflict arose.

One night, Ange was sitting at a table with her hand on the leg of a good-looking young soldier. She had been drinking beer all afternoon and was feeling no pain. She placed her head on the young man's shoulder, who hugged her return.

From the other side of the room, a large Corporal named Bethuel marched over to them and kicked the chair out from under the younger soldier.

The soldier bounced to his feet, yelled something, and punched Bethuel in the face.

'Big mistake,' Ange said and giggled.

Bethuel grabbed the younger man and hit him four times in the face. Ange jumped up and kicked Bethuel in the stomach, sending him flying backward.

Not quite done, she picked up a heavy wooden chair and smashed it against Bethuel's back as he tried to stand up.

From nowhere, she felt a heavy weight hit her from the side. She had been tackled and wrestled to the floor.

Normally she could break this type of grip, but her attacker countered her every move, until finally she knew she was pinned. She rolled on her back to view the man who had bested her. In her drunken state she failed to recognize him, so she headbutted the blurred face.

In a flash, the man headbutted her back twice as hard and Angelina Cohen was out for the night.

The man stood up and lifted her over his shoulder. Bethuel came charging back with the fury of a wounded bull. The man carrying Ange could see he wanted to kill her.

'Stand down, soldier!' the man yelled, and Bethuel stopped in his tracks. Bethuel was snorting in rage. His face was red, and his nostrils flared.

'Give her to me!' Bethuel raged.

'She is not herself,' the man said. 'If you knew what happened to her, you would understand.'

Something in the man's words reached Bethuel's animal brain. He threw up his arms in disgust, turned and walked away.

The man carried Ange out of the bar and threw her in the back of his car. When Ange came around, she was on the couch at home. She watched the man and her father talking at the dining room table.

It was then she recognized him. It was Lavie Katz! Her old platoon leader in the army ten years ago. Ange stood up and made her way to the table.

'I knew it was you as soon as I saw you,' Katz told her.

Ange was feeling sore and sorry. She touched her nose and wiped away the blood with the back of her hand, then looked at it.

Her father handed her a wet cloth and she cleaned herself up, then poured a beer.

'Nice headbutt, Katz,' she said. 'But then, you always did have a thick skull.'

'I know who's thick in the skull. Besides, you left your flank open,' Katz told her. 'Maybe you should give up bar fights, you're obviously you're not very good at them anymore.'

Ange gave him a tiger smile, making Katz sit back, ready to defend himself. This amused her so much she laughed out loud. It was a sound that sent shivers up her father's spine.

'Maybe you're right, Katz,' Ange conceded.

Alatan Cohen shrugged his shoulders and shook his head. He was at the end of his rope with his only beloved daughter.

'I have tried to help her,' Alatan told Katz. 'Can you talk some sense into her head before she gets herself killed?'

'I'll try,' Katz replied. 'But she's pretty stupid, you know?'

Alatan sighed again, got up, and went to bed.

Katz viewed Ange blandly. She had reverted to some kind of rebellious teenager, he guessed.

'Go to bed,' he told Ange. 'I'll come back in the morning and take you to breakfast.'

Ange said nothing and watched him leave. He was big and lean. She could see he was still a warrior.

The next day at seven a.m. sharp, Lavie Katz was back at the Cohen home. But he had lied to Ange. They were not going to breakfast; Katz had other plans.

'Get your boots on. We're going for a little run,' he told the sleepy and hungover Angelina.

The "little run" Katz had planned was actually an assault on The Hill, as it was known by the soldiers.

The Hill was a thousand-yard, thirty-degree incline ascent of ruts, gravel, and boulders. Then continued with a winding three-thousand yard descent on the back. The run finished with a light three-thousand yard jog back to the car. All up, it was two hours of pure misery.

Ange started to push back.

'If you don't get ready right now, we're through,' Katz told her. 'I'll leave you here to get drunk every night and fuck your way through the entire army base until some pissed off soldier cuts your throat.'

Katz's words resonated with a part of her brain she had locked away. He had told exactly what she needed to hear. This was her intervention. Her moment of clarity, she realized.

Ange could feel her heart start to beat again. The air suddenly felt clean, and she smiled a genuine smile for the first time in months.

'Fine,' she told him. 'But you know I'm going to beat your old ass.'

Katz smiled and nodded.

It was eighty degrees already, and getting hotter by the minute by the time Katz parked his car, and the pair commenced their ascent.

It took all of thirty seconds before Ange learned she was completely unfit.

It took another half an hour before she got her breathing under control, by which time Katz had left her far behind.

Not to be outdone and face humiliation at the hands of Katz, Ange dug deep and surged ahead. She could feel her heart pounding in her chest, beating hard like a blacksmith's hammer.

She focused on her outward breath to expel the carbon dioxide and suck in as much new air as possible to feed her dying body.

Push harder! she told herself. *Harder!*

At the top of the mountain, Ange knew she had depleted herself. She went down on her hands and knees, sucking in the dry desert air. But she felt more alive, as her body sweated out the alcohol toxins and cleared her mind of hateful thoughts.

'Cheaper than therapy,' she told herself.

Ange could hear Katz yelling obscenities at her, and she sprang to her feet. Her legs were energized, and her heart was still pounding like a machine. She began to run down the slope at full speed until she reached Katz. Then shoulder-charged the big man, knocking him to the ground.

'Crazy bitch!' Katz called after her. She laughed at him and kept running.

By the time Katz made it back to the car, he found a very different Angelina Cohen.

The girl at the car was covered in sweat and breathing hard, but she was smiling. Katz guessed she had not smiled like that for a long time.

The pair drove to a coffee shop and drank huge amounts of water, then ordered coffee.

'Catch me up,' Katz told her. 'What the fuck have you been doing for the last ten years?'

Angelina Cohen viewed the burly ex-soldier and suddenly a plan began to form in her mind. It was a plan to do a job she had been neglecting while she wallowed in self-pity.

'You wouldn't believe me if I told you,' Ange told him and shook her head.

'Hey, I have time. You can tell your old buddy Katz.'

Ange realized this was true. If there was anyone on the earth she could confide in, it was Katz.

So, she opened up and told Katz her story, focusing on recent events.

'My God! I can't believe you're still alive,' Katz told her. 'I'm really sorry about that Mack fellow. He sounds like one of the good guys.'

Ange shivered at hearing Mack's name again. She had to look away for a second, wondering if his memory would always cause a dark sickness to run through her.

'Yeah, he was one of the fucking good guys all right.' Ange said. 'But as we both know, there's no room for good guys in this world. Just a bunch of dead people who wanted to help people.'

Katz simply nodded. He had his own memory portfolio of dead soldiers and lost causes.

'But hey, the project was a risky gamble,' Ange told him. 'But it's still moving forward. They boys are still in Japan; in a place the Americans can't reach them.'

'What are we going to do now?' Katz asked solemnly. 'You know, us Israelis are very good at the revenge business.'

'We?' Ange asked. 'We are not going to do anything. This is not your fight.'

'I left the army three years ago and have been doing private security ever since. I am bored to death and need some fun in my life. I'm not ready for the pasture just yet.'

'This kind of fun will get you killed,' Ange told him.

'Fuck that!' Katz exclaimed. 'I can get killed right here. I know you're not going to let this lie. Do you have a plan?

'I have some ideas,' she conceded.

'Good. But if you do this, you'll need a team,' Katz told her. I have some ex-army buddies who might be available. Want to meet them?'

Ange viewed her old friend. He was a solid soldier, she knew. Solid and smart. But did she want to throw him off a cliff? She saw there was something in his eyes. Katz missed the fight, and men like him didn't care who they fought, if the cause was just.

'Who are these buddies of yours?' she asked.

'Oh, you'll like these guys,' Katz told her with a huge grin.

Three days later, Katz and Ange met the three ex-soldiers in a motel room, well off the tourist beat.

Ange had no idea if the names they gave were real, but that couldn't matter less.

They called themselves Eitan, Azrail, and Beria. Like Katz, they were now serving as private security contractors. A common role for men who gave their youth to Israel, but now knew what money was used for.

Ange briefed the men in broad strokes, not giving away too many details. She then asked if they wanted to learn more.

Like Katz, they were bored, but still battle-honed. They were making money, but it gave them no pleasure. The chance to do something of purpose again was very enticing.

All three men said they wanted to listen.

'I don't want the politicians, or the CIA,' Ange told them. 'They were mere pawns in this. I want the men who own the politicians and ordered us dead.'

She threw pictures of the US energy barons on the table.

'These men make trillions of dollars selling carbon-based fuel. For decades they have prevented the development of clean energy projects. They own all the politicians and murder anyone who jeopardizes their profits,' Ange told them.

One by one, the soldiers picked up the photos and examined them.

'These men killed my man and tried to kill everyone I love,' she said coldly.

The men viewed Ange and saw that the deal she offered was the real thing. Over the next few minutes, they asked a few specific questions until they were satisfied.

'How is this funded?' Azrail asked her.

Mack had left Ange a huge sum of money in his will. His company would be run by a board of trustees, leaving

Ange to live how she pleased. She judged there was no benefit in sharing these details yet.

'I have private backing,' she told them. 'If you agree to join me, you will receive one hundred thousand US dollars paid into your account immediately. This will cover your training and preparation stages. If, after that time, you choose to continue, you will be paid another two hundred thousand before we leave for the United States.'

She watched their reactions. The men were still listening.

'If the operation goes to plan,' Ange continued. 'You will be back in Israel within a month. There you will receive a bonus of another one hundred thousand.'

These men played a lot of poker. As such, nothing showed on their faces. One by one, they simply nodded their consent.

'Okay, this is what I've planned,' Ange began. 'If you think I've missed something, or you can spot an improvement, tell me. You are all going to have to look like rich Americans for a while. Cleaned-up and handsome.'

'Handsome?' Eitan scoffed. 'That counts you out Azrail. You look like a baboon that's been fucked by a donkey!'

'Watch your mouth, you little shit,' Azrail barked. 'Or I'll pull out my donkey to fuck you!'

The insults and threats flew back and forth for another few minutes, as the boys broke the tension.

Ange missed this. The bullshit before the battle with soldiers who were preparing to put their lives on the line.

'Who's our tech wizard?' Ange asked.

'I'm okay at it.' Katz put up his hand.

'Bullshit, man,' Eitan told him. 'Beria is twice as fast as you.'

Ange noted Beria was the quiet one. He didn't say much, but she could see he was always listening and thinking.

'What about it, Beria?' Ange asked him. 'Are you our tech guy?'

'I've been in and out of a few systems,' he said quietly. 'What do you need?'

'We're doing some bank hacks and money transfers,' Ange began. 'Social media hacking for live streaming, and radio comms interruption.'

'My twelve-year-old sister can do this,' Beria told her with a smile.

'Then what do we need you for?' Azrail asked. 'Go and get your fucking sister.' They all laughed.

'This is why I don't speak to you assholes,' Beria told them. 'You smell like camel pubis.'

They laughed again.

'Speaking of hair.' Ange changed the subject, 'You all need to let your hair grow. I need you all to look less like desert soldiers and more like Hollywood actors. You also need to practice our best American smiles. Do you know how to smile, Azrail?'

Ange got a chorus of 'fuck you' in return.

Las Vegas, Nevada, USA

Ange and her team arrived in Las Vegas one month before the Annual Energy Conference and Awards event. She explained to the soldiers that this event was the Academy Awards of the energy industry, attracting the key players from all the US energy sectors.

'Acclimation to a new environment is the key to success,' she told the men. 'A bunch of big hairy ex-soldiers, straight out of Israel will stand out like goat's balls.'

They knew this already but played along with her.

'You need to be comfortable, maybe even a little bored with your new surroundings,' she continued. 'One month should be enough time to knock off your sharp edges.'

'You know, Ange,' Beria began, 'some of these monkeys have never been accused of being sharp.'

He was rewarded with a smack on the back of his head.

Getting through the airport security was going to be an issue. Beria, with help from his friends in the Israeli security service, created new passports and IDs for them.

The team entered the US posing as desert agriculture farming consultants traveling through the southwest to exchange farm-related ideas and practices.

To match their cover, they hired a large SUV.

'Hey, I love this shit!' Eitan announced. 'I look like some kind of fucking cowboy.'

'No swearing, okay,' Ange admonished him. 'Americans believe in Jesus, so never swear near them and certainly not at them.'

'Who the fuck is this Jesus guy?' Eitan asked. 'Does he play American football?' Azrail smacked him on the back of the head.

'You are an idiot, Eitan,' Azrail told him. 'Did you know that?

'At least I know who my father is,' Eitan told him.

'I know who my father is,' Azrail said. 'He is the guy who visited your mother every night.'

'Do we have to listen to this shit for a whole month?' Katz asked Ange.

'I'm afraid so,' Ange told him with a broad smile.

Morale was high, Ange mused. But then morale was always high in the beginning of an operation. Let's hope it can last the whole month with a bunch of hard men living in close proximity and not a whole lot to do, she thought to herself.

Katz started the SUV.

'Here we go, boys!' Ange announced. 'Off to the motel, then I'm taking you idiots shopping. You are about to become my glamour boys.'

The team checked into a very tidy four-star motel, where they were all were assigned a shared room.

Ange knew it was good practice to team the men into pairs, as they were conditioned to work and live in groups.

A soldier alone in a room at night in a city like Las Vegas could end in trouble.

The motel Ange picked was comfortable, but not swanky. If anyone was tracking them, she wanted to give the appearance they were not rich, and they were not hiding. To be in plain sight, but humble. Just like a group of international farm consultants.

After they settled in and showered, the team met in the downstairs lobby.

'Next stop; the mall for new clothes,' Ange told them. 'Beria, I need you to make a list of the IT equipment you will need.'

'I have the list already,' he told her. 'Just get me to a computer store.'

The transformation went much smoother than Ange had hoped. The men had their game faces on and were rapidly transforming into American shoppers.

They all gave into her on clothing and hairstyle selections. Being fit and lean, they could wear almost anything that looked stylish around the pool, and in the bar of a swanky Las Vegas hotel.

Beria had found a large computer store and came back with boxes of equipment.

By the end of the afternoon, they gathered for an early dinner. Ange had had them on the hop all day and they were hungry. Steaks, fries, and salads were wolfed down, followed by cold frothy beer.

'Now for the bad news,' Ange told them.

They looked up.

'New clothes will help, but you all still look like soldiers. Tomorrow we are all off to the spa.'

'What the fuck?' Azrail almost choked on his beer.

'Your hands and faces are too rough,' she said. 'I need you boys to be soft and pretty for me.'

'How long is this spa trip?' Etain asked. 'They will need a month to make Azrail pretty!'

Then Beria picked his moment.

'Are they also miracle workers?' he asked.

'If this mission goes bad, I am leaving both of you here to die,' Azrail told them.

He threw a bread roll at Etain. This of course, started a bread war.

'Stop!' Ange yelled at them. 'It's like taking children out! Now drink your beer quietly!'

They laughed and clinked their beer jugs. 'Here's to us and fuck all of you!' Etain declared.

'Fuck you all!' they chorused.

The Annual Energy Conference — Aria Hotel, Las Vegas

The woman stood near the main entrance of the hotel wearing a faded baseball cap that protested a war that most people had long forgotten.

Her baggy jeans and a nondescript black T-shirt ensured she would not attract anyone's attention. Her hi-vis vest read "Press", providing cover for her to film the energy barons' limousines as they arrived.

As a hunter viewed its prey, she balefully etched the faces of her targets into her memory as they slumped their corpulent masses out of the cars.

It had been a long road back for Angelina Cohen.

After the bombing and death of her lover, she had recovered quickly from her physical injuries. Yet her emotional wounds remained raw and open.

In past times, when struck by adversity, her lion roared and she killed rapidly, without the need for complex planning.

Today, her lion had stopped roaring. Instead, it stood still and quiet beside her. Alert and watchful. Ready to kill the second the command was given. Ange planned her justice without emotion, or the need for expedience.

This new approach made Angelina Cohen twice as dangerous.

Her forged letters of appointment and international press card told its readers she was a freelance reporter for a Middle Eastern finance magazine franchise.

The team had transitioned from their old motel to the Aria the week before. There they trained and rehearsed for their operation. Every day they worked out in the gym, practiced their drills, then acted like carefree Vegas tourists.

Many of the energy barons had arrived at the hotel and were due to appear at an industry press conference in The Palms conference room.

The conference organizers were happy to have Ange as part of the Press Corp and issued her ID and pass tags.

Ange was ushered into the conference room and directed where to stand. There was long table at the end of the room where lights and microphones were set up.

Ange dressed carefully for this phase of the mission. Her dress goal was expensive but business-like.

She wore a white silk business suit that was form fitting, but not provocatively so. Her shoes were Jimmy Choos that took her height to just under six foot. She pulled her long black hair back in a practical ponytail and wore black framed glasses.

When her team saw her, they switched from brutish, overconfident soldiers to coy schoolboys.

'Calm down you idiots,' she told them. 'It's just a costume.'

The barons filed into the conference room and took up their assigned seating.

Ange had been working her mantras hard all week. In her training as a Mossad spy, she practiced neurolinguistic method acting.

The key was self-talk. What you said to yourself is what you believe. More importantly, how you act.

She had to erase all the hatred she felt for these men to get the job done. If she felt hatred, hatred would emanate from her like a warning beacon. She needed these men to and want her, and she knew they were not easily fooled.

You don't become the leader of a multibillion-dollar empire without developing a finely tuned intuition. The Energy Barons could read the slightest incongruent vibration from a person a mile away.

Ange's assigned position was just fifteen feet from the barons' table. A perfect place for them all to get a good look at her.

She stood square on to the table with her legs slightly apart. Every minute or so she changed her stance subtly by placing one leg forward, then a twist to get an item from her bag, and back again.

She knew that first impressions were everything, and she needed the men to become stimulated enough to reach out to her.

Once the conference started, questions and answers passed back and forth. The room was small, and the heat began to rise.

Ange asked her question about drilling potential in the Russian permafrost. It was a worthy question, and good enough to gain the barons' full attention.

She looked at each of them in turn, making direct eye contact. Just enough to capture their attention, but she made no overt gestures. The art was in the subtlety, she knew. A little taste, but nothing obvious.

As the conference wound down, Ange made her way to the exit and into the corridor. She counted to thirty, then walked past the door the barons were set to leave by.

Her timing was perfect.

As the barons exited into the narrow hall, Ange walked past them. The first man through the door was Don Theck, CEO of Southern United Coal.

In his life, Don Theck had consumed quantities of fried chicken, mashed potatoes, and peach cobbler that would stun a small horse. These culinary selections settled mostly in his midsection, much to the dismay of his tailor and the disgust of his wife. Combined with his thinned out greasy hair and sun-damaged skin, Don Theck was a hard man to miss in a crowd.

On this day, Theck was treated to an up-close view of Angelina Cohen as she strode past just a few feet away. She was so close he could smell her fresh perfume, and felt a breeze touch his face generated by her athletic body.

Theck moaned with involuntary ecstasy, loud enough for Ange to hear him. She performed a quick flick-back glance and smiled at him.

That's all you get for now; she mused and strode away toward the nearest elevator.

Back in the team suite, Ange went straight to her room. When she reappeared, she was wearing gym gear.

Beria asked her how it went.

'Oh, you know. I guess we'll see,' she reported. 'But I feel like I'm covered in shit.'

'Where are you going?' he asked.

'To the gym. I need to burn the evil out,' Ange told him as she walked out the door.

The boys understood; their girl needed heavy weights, sweat, and pain.

An Undisclosed Location, Japan

The Japanese authorities deemed it advantageous to keep Lucas, John, and Kurt away from the bomb site investigations and other harmful distractions. They were also now aware of the lengths the US government will go to stop the free energy programme.

A new site was found in an old underground cold war bunker complex near Tokyo city. The site was off the grid and all roads in were blocked. All the equipment lost in bombing was reacquired and delivered to the new location. Replacement personnel were transported in under a total security blackout.

After Mack's death, the Japanese government adopted ownership of the project, in partnership with Mack's board of trustees. They made the young scientists a very lucrative offer with ongoing royalties, including full public credit for their work.

Physically, the boys had recovered from their minor wounds. Emotionally, however, they remained hollow and fragile.

The Japanese knew Sam Kimora was their closest friend in Japan and they assigned her to help them through their transition and recovery.

'All three are having trouble sleeping,' their therapist told Sam. 'They are not eating well and two of them have recurring head colds.'

'What do you suggest?' Sam asked.

'They are your friends,' the doctor said. 'You will need to be close to them. Encourage them to talk and just listen. Show them they have a friend they can trust.'

'You know I have no training as a counsellor. I don't know how much good I will do,' Sam told him.

'It's no big mystery,' the therapist assured her. 'Time, along with unconditional support are the only two things that can heal in cases of loss.'

Sam met up with the boys in the dining mess.

'I wish Ange was here,' Lucas said. 'We hardly got to speak to her after the, you know…'

'I miss her too,' Sam agreed. 'Don't worry, I know we'll see her again soon.'

'Ange is a survivor. I'm sure she's okay,' Kurt said. 'It just sucks not knowing where she is or what she's doing.'

'The only way I see this deal playing out is that,' John began, 'we get the job done, then we're out of here. What are you guys going to do with your share of the money?'

'The money?' Lucas asked. 'I hope we get a chance to spend it.'

'Do you really think the US government still want us dead after the tech has been released?' Kurt asked. 'I mean, that will be pretty pointless, wouldn't it?'

'I guess so,' Lucas told him. 'Anyway, the new antenna is being installed, and the tests on the frequency algorithm look good. Kurt, are you ready to hook up your turbine?'

Kurt based his turbine generator on Nikola Tessler's water turbine design; a small-gap, multi-rotor machine that spun at incredible speeds. The problem with Tesla's one hundred-year-old original design was overheating. The turbine was just too efficient for its time.

Kurt's turbine did not suffer these problems. He used superconducting magnetic bearings and liquid cooled titanium rotors.

'I think we are ready to jump ahead and perform a multi-stage test on the frequency resonance chamber and the turbine power drawdown,' Lucas told them.

'Fuck it! I agree,' Kurt announced. 'Let's see what this baby can do.'

'I'll hook up the OAC (omni antenna collector) to the FRR (frequency resonance rationalizer),' Lucas said. 'Kurt, you'll need to be johnny-on-the-spot with the turbine actuator. We have no idea how efficient this thing is, and I don't want to get fried.'

Kurt looked down at his turbine and crossed his fingers.

'I'll have my hand on the kill switch, don't worry,' he told them.

'Okay, folks,' Lucas said. 'Take us to a hundred watts.'

Over the next three hours, the boys ran tests on a range of conservative power settings.

After several attempts and some fine tuning of their instruments, Lucas, John, and Kurt were able to disrupt the quantum fields in their resonance chamber and draw out pure electromagnetic energy in highly predictable amounts.

'Are we ready for the big test?' Lucas asked.

The team was silent. The "big test" was to draw power in the megawatt range. New York city consumed eight thousand megawatts per hour. If their machine could do anything like that, it would change the world forever.

'We need to clear the lab,' John warned. 'I won't be responsible for killing all these people.'

'Agreed,' Lucas said. 'Everyone! Listen up. We need you to clear the lab right now. Lock the blast doors on your way out please.'

The Japanese technicians were reluctant at first but could see Lucas was deadly serious.

'That includes you two,' Lucas told John and Kurt.

They both gave Lucas their answers with a flurry of insults.

Lucas knew he'd lost the argument.

'Fine,' he said. 'Kurt, double check the breakers and voltage vent. I don't want this thing blowing back into here.'

'Okay, showtime. Give me one megawatt on the dial,' Lucas instructed.

Kurt's turbine silently began its rotations while they watched the dials climb. As the power approached the megawatt range a blue hue began to emit from the resonance chamber, while the turbine produced a gentle hum.

For the first time in history, mankind had tapped into vacuum energy as the young men synchronized their machine with the latent power of the universe.

'Turbine revolutions are at twenty thousand rpms, and the conductors are stable. Heat readings are all green. Bearings are all green,' Kurt announced. 'My God, we are actually doing this. We're producing one megawatt of power!'

On top of the mountain, far above the lab, a tall metal pole vented the power into the sky in the form of electromagnetic streaks of lightning.

'Let's try to maintain this for one hour,' Lucas said.

As the time crept by, the boys silently monitored their instruments. Every piece of hardware they designed worked exactly as predicted, producing a continuous one megawatt of power for the whole hour.

'Okay,' Lucas called. 'Wind her down.'

When the generator closed down the group went quiet. The rapid development of their machine had caught them by surprise. After years of planning and experimenting their machine actually worked

In just one live test, their free energy machine had made redundant the burning of coal, oil, and gas. The fossil fuel global energy barons were about to lose their stranglehold on the people of Earth.

More importantly, the Earth would have a chance to recover from over one hundred years of industrial and vehicular smog. A vast amount of greenhouse gases would soon be eliminated.

The boys knew they had a few short minutes to celebrate their accomplishments before all hell broke loose and their lives would change forever.

'I've read about moments like these,' Lucas said. 'When they were building the atom bomb at Los Alamos in 1945, it was all heads-down and work. Then the day came to test it, and someone asked if the atomic chain reaction would ignite the hydrogen in the sky. They hadn't even considered that. They were only focused on the job at hand.'

'That's where we are right now,' John affirmed. 'We have created a world without the need to burn fossil fuels. But in doing so, we have made millions of people redundant.'

'The economic effects of this machine will be catastrophic for many people,' Lucas began. 'But on the other hand, computers, the internet, robotics in manufacturing, and global trade also caused mass unemployment.'

'And economies adjusted, and we moved on,' Kurt finished his sentence.

'That's right.' Lucas smiled.

'Unless some politician comes along and fucks this up; our machine will go online just in time to save the planet,' John told them.

Fortunately for them, they were far beyond the reach of the people who wanted to kill this project. The host government Mackenzie James chose to harbour the project were desperate for free energy, and nothing could stop them now.

It was one of life's perfect symbiotic arrangements.

The Aria Hotel, Las Vegas

The doorbell sounded in the suite.

Ange answered it to find a well-dressed young man who introduced himself as Jason. He informed Ange that he worked for Donald Theck, owner of Southern United Coal, and that Mr Theck would like to offer Ange passes to all the conference social events.

He handed Ange an embossed packet that contained invitations to the premier cocktail party, the following dinner, and a gold pass to the nightclub.

'Please understand,' Jason said. 'These invitations are extremely rare and only go to VIP guests. Mr Theck would be personally honoured if you would attend.'

Ange walked back in to the living room holding up the passes.

'Well, that worked,' Azrail said.

Ange nodded and sighed. This was her moment.

Six p.m. that night, Angelina Cohen had dressed in her cocktail party costume. She wore a fun and flirty lime green Versace strappy gathered dress with a string of fine pearls. Her shoes were white Givenchy, and she carried a glossy white Gucci pouch.

They voted Etain as the prettiest boy in the team to be her escort.

'You scrub up okay for a scrappy retired soldier,' Ange told him.

'And you, my lady, are almost pretty enough to be my date!' Etain said with a flurry, getting himself into character.

The pair chuckled, while the other men looked on with envy. They had to cool their heels until the next phase of the operation.

Ange and Etain made their way to the cocktail party in the Alibi Lounge. Ange timed it to arrive thirty minutes late. Her guess was the barons would have at least two drinks under their belts by then.

They flashed their pass and were invited straight in.

Ange led Etain into the centre of the room, where she could see at least three of the barons seated on lounges. She made a show of looking for somewhere to sit so everyone could get a good look at her.

Satisfied, she led Etain to the bar.

They ordered cocktails and made pretend small talk until Jason showed up again.

'Mr Theck would like to extend his compliments,' Jason told Ange. 'He would like to invite you to join him at his lounge.'

Jason motioned toward the lounge where Don Theck was seated. He then viewed Etain.

'Mr Theck made it clear the invitation was for you only,' Jason said.

Etain stood and buttoned his jacket. He smiled at Jason in a manner that clearly said, 'Fuck you.'

'I've got to finish that article,' Etain told Ange. 'I'll see you tomorrow.'

Ange picked up her drink and followed Jason to the lounge, where Don Theck stood and introduced himself.

Ange locked eyes with Theck and shook his hand firmly, ensuring he could feel as much of her skin as possible. She gave his hand the mildest of all squeezes and held it for a moment longer than was necessary. Theck blushed and a bead of sweat formed on his upper lip.

Ange gave a coy little smile and looked away.

That was easy, she told herself.

Theck's entourage was a mix of three middle-aged business types and two young women in cocktail dresses. The men looked pleased that Ange had joined their party, but the young women looked less than impressed.

'Please, sit and have a glass of champagne,' Theck said. 'Tell us all about yourself.'

Ange did her rehearsed spiel about being a journalist, then asked Theck about his company.

Theck was more than happy to comply. Ange asked him all the right questions, while providing the man with complimentary responses. Ange had the skills to keep powerful men engaged for hours. If, and when, she chose to.

But after five minutes, Ange performed her pullback. This was a psychological manoeuvre designed to create heightened desire in her target.

'You'll have to excuse me,' she announced. 'I have a publishing deadline.' She stood and picked up her handbag.

Theck was aghast.

'You can't go yet,' he pleaded. 'You just arrived!'

'A girl has to work,' Ange told him.

Theck was mortified.

'You must join us for dinner,' he insisted.

Ange smiled coyly and nodded.

'Do you have your invitation?' he asked.

'Yes, I do,' Ange purred sweetly and smiled. Theck had swallowed the final barb on the hook. The man was entranced.

Ange made a show of turning and walking away. She put a very subtle sway in her hips and some catwalk breeze in her stride.

One hour and fifteen minutes later, Ange was at the restaurant where Jason, once again, escorted her to Don Theck's table. Theck stood and warmly welcomed her, insisting Ange be seated next to him and poured her a glass of champagne.

Ange shuddered when Theck touched her back as she sat. Control yourself and feel the joy, was her mantra for the evening.

The night went as expected, as Ange played her hand perfectly. She chatted with Theck then focused on a few other guests, making him wait his turn.

She refocused on him, touching his arm when making a point, and laughed at all his dumb jokes. She drank enough champagne to give Theck the impression she was happy to get drunk with him.

She then slid her chair closer to his, until Theck could feel the side of her leg against his. Ange, in turn, felt his body brace, knowing he was becoming aroused.

Finally, when he could take no more, Theck pulled Ange to one side and whispered in her ear.

'My wife and kids are in the hotel and I need to get back to my room at some point,' he said. 'Is there anywhere we can go for a private drink?'

Ange faked surprise, then gave him a cheeky smile and nodded.

'My room is empty,' she whispered and slid her room card into his sweaty palm.

'Give me five minutes,' Ange whispered. 'A girl needs to freshen up.' Theck took a deep breath and nodded like a schoolboy on prom night.

Ange stood and made her apologies to her new dinner friends. She promised to see them all again and left the restaurant. When she was clear, Ange made the call.

'Five minutes. Get ready.'

Right on cue, the team heard the room door open. A man's voice was calling to Ange. They had turned the lights down low and were hiding out of sight.

'Come in, Donny!' Ange called from the lounge. 'I've poured us a whisky.'

Theck emerged from the shadows and entered the dimly lit room. He saw Ange seated on the lounge with a whiskey in her hand and a second glass on the table.

Theck smiled and came all the way into the room.

'My God,' he said. 'You are a beauty!'

Ange smiled at him in a way that made him tremble. He picked up his glass and drank.

As he moved toward her, the room suddenly went out of focus. Inexplicably, everything began to swirl, and his legs folded beneath him.

Theck's last thought was that he was having a stroke.

'Not now,' he moaned as he fell to the floor. The team immediately went to work.

Dressed as hotel employees, they heaved Theck into a body bag, then hoisted his corpulent mass into a laundry trolley. They covered him in linen, threw their luggage and equipment into a second trolley, and made their way to a service elevator. On their way out, Ange wiped the door handle and the glass Theck had been holding.

Five minutes later their SUV drove out of the hotel parking lot and onto the strip, heading toward a rented house in the Las Vegas suburbs.

The owners lived interstate and had listed the house for rent on the web. They were very happy to receive a large bond and a month's rent upfront.

The SUV entered the large garage where the door rolled down behind them. Don Theck, the mighty CEO of America's largest and most corrupt coal producing conglomerate had disappeared from the world.

The team prepped the house. They closed all the curtains and set Theck up on a chair in the middle of the living room. He was bound to the chair with heavy plastic ties at the feet and wrists. Thick industrial tape bound his waist and chest.

Beria set up his laptop and camera, then connected to the internet via his satellite-linked wireless modem. He used a foreign web service that was virtually untraceable.

Azrail and Katz put down plastic drop mats while Etain gathered the remainder of the materials they would need.

'Let the show begin!' Ange told them.

At two a.m. Andrea Theck woke from a shallow sleep to find her bed was empty. She immediately assumed Don was sleeping with some other woman elsewhere in the hotel.

She knew all about his "talent scout" pimp Jason who he paid very well to solicit unfortunate young girls for her husband's amusement. She shuddered in disgust at the thought of them enduring the weight of her fat, ugly husband while he slobbered all over them.

Andrea shook off the thought and took a hot shower.

Before leaving Israel, Beria used his Mossad connections to gain vials of some very specific drugs. He had the tranquillizer that was currently debilitating Theck, and the antidote. He had also obtained sodium thiopenta, also called sodium pentothal. This drug leads to synaptic inhibition, decreased neuronal excitability, and if overdosed, anaesthesia.

Beria injected Theck with the tranquilizer antidote. Ange stood and waited as Theck began to come around. She could see he was gaining awareness of his surroundings and nodded to Beria to inject the sodium thiopenta.

She stood directly in front of him smiling down at the man. She watched his eyes roll as she stroked his head.

'Hi, Donny. How are you feeling?'

Theck looked up and focused on her face.

'Ange? Is that you? What the hell happened?'

'Oh, Donny. You fell asleep. But it's going to be okay. I'll take care of you.'

She dropped to her knees to be at the same eye level as him and soothed his face with a moist towel.

This made him smile.

'You're so pretty, Ange. I think I love you.'

'I love you too, Donny, but your office called and they urgently need your bank account numbers. What are your bank account numbers, Donny?'

Theck was feeling very fine. His brain was swimming in warm pool of bliss, and all his inhibitions were gone.

'Which bank accounts do you need?' Theck asked, then giggled like a teenager.

'All of them, Donny,' Ange purred for him. 'I need all of them.'

Beria was poised at his laptop in the corner of the room and began typing as Theck revealed the names of banks and corresponding account numbers.

Ange then asked for the passwords and Theck gave them straight up.

'Start the camera,' she told Beria.

Beria had set up a Facebook page specifically for this moment. He had sent the link to all the major broadcasting networks in the US, Europe, and Asia.

He turned on his camera and began the live feed, giving Ange the thumbs up. Ange had moved to her left, allowing the mounted camera to focus on Don Theck's face.

'I love the President, Donny,' Ange began. 'You and the other energy barons did such a good job getting him elected.'

'Thank you, Ange. Can I kiss you?'

'In a little while. But first, I want to know how you got him elected?' Theck smiled boyishly.

'Anything for you, Ange.'

Over the next twenty minutes, Theck described how he and the other energy barons had set up election super PACs and injected millions of untraceable dollars into them. How that money paid for thousands of media advertisements and bribed several top-rated right wing media personalities.

'What about social media, Donny?' Ange asked. 'How did that work?'

'I don't really know much about that,' Theck began. 'We paid a firm to do all that for us. They bought huge amounts of personal data and channelled hate messages to the more impressionable and gullible demographics of America.'

'What messages did you send, Donny?'

'Oh, you know, the usual right-wing stuff. Guns are good. Free medical is communism. Jews control the banks and immigrants steal all the jobs. Oh, climate change is a fraud, and Democrats are communists and traitors.'

Don Theck laughed out loud. He was thoroughly enjoying himself. He relished the memory of how easy it was to sell all these lies to Republican voters and the President's fan base.

'We even invented QAnon! No one thought it would work. But they didn't know how stupid rednecks really are. I did. I knew!'

'Which broadcasters did you bribe?'

Ange waited patiently while Theck named names and gave details of the cash amounts the barons paid out. She checked again with Beria to ensure everything was being recorded.

Beria smiled broadly and gave the thumbs up again. His live streaming video was up to one thousand views already and the numbers were climbing.

'Did you hear about Mackenzie James and the three scientists who were building the free energy machine? They went to Japan, didn't they?'

Theck smiled broadly and began nodding like a dog.

'You don't have to worry about them, Ange. We got rid of them for you.'

'Thank you, Donny. I love you so much. But tell me, who else helped you?' Theck began to laugh again.

'Come on, Donny, tell me.'

'All of us! All the energy guys, the CIA, and the President. Do you know how dumb the President really is? My God, we've elected some beauties over the years, but this guy is dumber than a hat full of monkey piss.'

Ange stood up and stood beside Beria. She saw the views had reached five thousand and the click counter was racing to keep up.

'Make copies of the video before they shut us down,' she told him.

Beria went to work as Ange watched the whole video show. It was all there.

'The money?' Ange asked.

'I've moved it all into our accounts in the Caymans, Panama, Mexico, and Moscow. In about two minutes it will all be diverted to Switzerland.

'Contact the Swiss and instruct them to disburse it the second it arrives,' Ange told him. 'Looks like our charities will be having a very good year.'

'Piece of cake,' Beria said with a big smile.

'You really are our tech guy,' Ange bent down and kissed his cheek, making the man blush.

Theck was calling for Ange to come back. Instead, Ange called for Etain, Azrail, and Katz.

'Drown this fucking rat for me,' she told them.

The men came into the room with two five-gallon drums of water. Katz kicked Theck's chair over, sending him sprawling backward onto the plastic sheet.

With Theck on his back and legs in the air, the men covered his face with a towel.

'You look thirsty, asshole,' Katz told him.

Theck was now completely confused, unable to comprehend his situation as the water began to pour into his mouth and nose.

'You've killed a lot of good people, Donny,' Ange told him. 'You've broken American democracy, poisoned the air, and attempted to stop the science of light energy.'

Don Theck coughed against the water, but couldn't stop laughing.

'This is your judgement day, Donny,' Ange told him. 'And you are not going to die quickly.'

Ange nodded at Katz.

As the water flowed onto Theck's face, he tried to hold his breath. But that only delayed the inevitable.

He finally took a breath, and the water began to fill his lungs. The old myth that one experiences a sense of euphoria when drowning eluded Don Theck as his lungs began to burn.

With all his humour exhausted, Don Theck died badly. He died in pain, and in a state of sheer terror.

Ange watched the process without emotion. This was justice. It was revenge for her lover, and payback for a lifetime of pure evil.

At ten a.m. that morning, the hotel Kid's Club people arrived and Andrea Theck's children went off for their day of activities. Don Theck had not returned to the room.

Good, Andrea thought. *I hope he never comes back.*

She dressed in her gym clothes and hit the machines. She took her time, enjoying every minute away from her husband. When finished, she took a soothing spa before heading back to the room.

When she re-entered the room, the clock showed eleven thirty a.m. Minutes later the doorbell rang. She opened the door to find Jason.

'Excuse me, ma'am. Don is late for a meeting and he's not answering his phone.'

Andrea Theck immediately knew something was wrong. Theck's phone was never turned off and he always scurried back to the room, no matter what he'd been up to.

'Where was he last night?' she asked.

'Sorry, ma'am, I'm not sure.'

'Don't fuck with me, you little weasel!' Andrea Theck yelled at him. 'Tell me right the fuck now!'

Jason knew he was damned both ways, so he took a middle route.

'The last time I saw him was at the dinner.'

'And which whore was he at dinner with?' Andrea spat.

'Just business colleagues, ma'am,' Jason lied.

'Bullshit! Call security and find the lump of shit,' she told him.

'Yes ma'am.'

Minutes later, hotel security came to the Theck's room and interviewed Jason. He told them about Ange the reporter, and how Theck was very interested in her.

With the help of video surveillance, they found Ange's room number. They searched it, but it was completely empty.

Security then played back the hallway footage of her floor. They watched in horror as Theck went into the room at ten fifteen p.m. Then twenty minutes later, a woman and four men came out pushing two laundry carts.

Don Theck did not.

The hotel manager had since placed himself in charge of the search for Theck. The last thing he needed were blaring headlines, declaring a VIP guest had been abducted from his hotel.

In his twenty-five-year career, the manager had worked in hotels in Europe and the Middle East. What he had watched on the videos had all the hallmarks of a professional abduction. It did not take long for him to reach the only possible conclusion.

The man sighed and called the police.

Within an hour of that call, after witness interviews, and further examination of hotel surveillance video, LVPD detectives broadcast an APB for a black SUV, driven by four men and a woman with its tag numbers.

The distorted images of the suspect's faces were generated and sent to every hotel and motel in the Greater Las Vegas area. Train stations, bus terminals, car rentals, and Airports were alerted.

All these actions, of course, were several hours too late. It was then an officer ran into the hotel security office.

'You need to see this!' she told the Chief of Police and opened her laptop.

The police team stood and watched the recorded video of Don Theck's confession. The Chief knew at once a bomb was about to go off.

'Get me the FBI right now!' he called.

The Interview

'Mackenzie James is dead,' Rowland Smith began formally. 'You and your team were in Japan and about to release your energy project to the world, and the media was broadcasting Don Theck's confession video infinitum. Did anything come from all that corruption evidence?'

'Not really,' Lucas said matter-of-factly. 'The right-wing media created a convenient set of alternative facts; stating that Don Theck was a drug addict and in-debt to various cartels. That he'd planned the whole thing. But Theck was dead, and he was the only witness.'

'And the other energy barons? How did they react?'

'As you know,' Lucas began. 'Theck's assailants were never caught and are still out there. Will they hunt down the other barons? Who knows? But I'm sure they'll be looking over their shoulders for a very long time.'

'The hotel video clearly shows four men and a woman,' Smith said. 'Reports state they were using some kind of invisible face paint that dupes facial recognition software. They say the kidnapping, and what transpired later, was military in its precision.'

'The energy barons have been operating an organised programme of environmental destruction, election tampering, and political corruption for decades. Perhaps a group of ex-military American patriots took it upon themselves to restore some justice. Who knows?'

'Or, it was someone who had a personal stake in your clean energy programme,' Smith offered. 'Someone who lost her lover in the bombing of the Japanese lab? Perhaps a female with a military past?'

'As you know, Rowland, I am not a federal prosecutor,' Lucas told him. For me to speculate on these events would be superfluous.'

'Okay, I'll accept that for now. Let's get back to the business at hand. When will your free energy machine be released?'

Lucas laughed.

'That's the good part!' Lucas told him.

The National Stadium — Tokyo, Japan

Lucas, John and Kurt were seated centre field in the massive stadium built for the 2021 Olympic games.

They were surrounded by hundreds of scientists and invited government representatives from every corner of the globe. The remainder of the seats were placed in a lottery for the general public. Millions of people wanted to take part in this historical event.

The only country not represented was America. The Japanese made a public point of not inviting them and made it very clear they had no part to play in the world-changing science.

On the field was a multi-stage array of lights, huge display screens, neon signs, electric car charging stations, electric water heaters, and factory machines.

In the centre was a box the size of a small car with a short, round-topped fiberglass dome that was covered in an antenna array.

'Welcome ladies and gentlemen, scientists, and world leaders!' the announcer said (in Japanese, then in English). 'You are here to witness the first live demonstration of the zero-point energy, quantum vacuum machine. What you are about to see will power our world without the burning of fossil fuels, or the creation of any waste matter.'

'For over a century, particle physicists studied the theory of destabilizing zero-point energy fields, yet as you have already learned, even more powerful human business and political forces prevented this research from bearing fruit.

'The demonstration you are about to see is to honour the memories of those brave scientists who died in the attempt to bring this free, clean, abundant energy to you, the people.

'Without delay, I will ask the men who risked everything to come forward and activate the device. Lucas Harding, John Carol, and Kurt Hangle.'

The three scientists made their way to a platform facing the audience. In front of them was a lectern supporting a touchpad computer. The application for operating the device had a series of activation buttons and a system performance display.

'This project is dedicated to the memory of Mackenzie James and the Japanese scientists who gave their lives to bring the world clean energy,' Lucas said into the microphone.

With that, Lucas typed in the activation code and touched the start key.

A few feet away they heard their machine hum into life as energy was drawn from the resonance chamber.

Lucas nodded to Kurt. 'She's all yours, big boy.'

Kurt touched the key and his turbine spun into life.

Seconds later, the LCD graph showed it was spinning at ten thousand rpm, generating a constant stream of one megahertz AC electricity.

Lucas viewed his three companions.

'Show time!' he said with a huge grin.

He touched another button, and the light show began.

The audience watched in awe as the tiny generator lit up hundreds of lights, TV screens, and powered a collection of large industrial machines. In the centre of the field, water boiled in huge glass vats, sending clouds of vapor into the air.

For their crescendo, a small army of robots stood and performed a dance to Lady Gaga's "Poker face", complete with a laser show backdrop.

Over fifty thousand people in the stadium, and over a billion people watching live in their homes, businesses and universities around the world were completely spellbound.

'Check your phones everyone!' Lucas called into the microphone. 'All these machines you are watching are being powered by Wi-Fi energy, and you are getting a free phone charge!'

The stadium erupted again.

Las Vegas

After killing Don Theck, the team abandoned their SUV in a private business car park near the old Vegas strip. They removed their travel kits and initiated the timers on two petrol bombs inside the car.

From two blocks away, they heard a muffled boom after the flames incinerated all physical evidence of their crimes. Ange had dyed her hair blonde, dressed in jeans, a ranch shirt, and wore a cowboy hat.

The team said their farewells and one by one, they disappeared into the crowd of Vegas holiday makers. With new IDs, they hired individual cars and drove into the night. By the time the FBI launched their APB, there was nothing left to find. The team were ghosts.

Over the next twenty-four hours, they had all left America from separate international airports within the US Southwest. Using fake credit cards, IDs, and passports they purchased airline tickets for destinations around the globe, including Rio, Sydney, Bangkok, and Rome.

In time, they would all return to Israel as rich men, but as Ange knew, they would have done this job for free. As professional soldiers, they were all practiced in keeping secrets. It was a skill that did not challenge them in the slightest.

Ange, however, did not go back to Israel.

She caught an indirect flight to Tokyo with many stop-overs in between.

In the air, she had watched several broadcasts of her three scientists demonstrating their free energy machine. The follow up scientific reviews were glowing and the machine performed far beyond anyone's expectations.

Thank God, she marvelled with great relief.

Sitting there alone on the plane, Ange thought of Mack. This was his dream. His plan. And despite the horrendous set-back, her boys made it work. How incredible they all were, she thought.

Yet, Mack was not here to celebrate. He was not here, and she was alone. A tear formed and spilled down her face. It was a tear for Mack. She knew how much he loved her, with so much respect and dignity. Her tear was the last trace of him for now, until she would cry for him again on another day.

She looked out the window and watched the clouds roll by below her. Ange sensed Mack was out there somewhere, in the clouds with her on her final journey.

The Las Vegas police found the SUV, but little evidence remained in the ashes from the fire.

The FBI attempted to track the SUV's movements via uploaded data from the onboard navigation. But the team had disabled that on day one. With few leads to go on, they resorted to traffic surveillance footage.

Two days later, they watched the SUV turn off the 595 and onto Sahara Drive West, where it disappeared into The Lakes district. They cross-checked the area with a recent "homes for rent" web search and compiled a hit list.

There were ten rented homes in the area to search. By four p.m. that afternoon, after three days of ninety-degree heat, they found the bloated body of Don Theck.

Agent Kelly Poliski and Special Agent Nick Scanlan, were the first through the door. Both were hit with a plume of stench that reeled them backward. They raced to open windows, attempting to control their convulsive nausea.

It was too late. Poliski vomited first, quickly followed by Scanlan. They regained their composure and began the investigation. After a preliminary search, they found a thumb drive in an envelope labelled "FBI".

Poliski retrieved her laptop from the car and read the data from the drive. It was a multiple tab excel spreadsheet with labels that included: "Super PAC payments", "Media Co. deposits", "Political fundraisers".

It showed vast sums of money being deposited in offshore accounts and those same accounts being accessed by nefarious individuals. Including individuals who currently work in the White House.

Poliski showed it to Scanlan.

Nick Scanlan knew at once this material had ramifications that far exceeded his pay grade. He closed the laptop and thought for a second.

'We're out of here,' he told Poliski. 'This has to get back to HQ, right now.'

He handed over the investigation to another special agent, and the pair raced back to the Las Vegas field office.

An hour later, he and Kelly Poliski were on an FBI jet heading to Washington.

FBI Headquarters — 935 Pennsylvania Avenue, Washington DC.

FBI Director Lew Krane read the documents for a second time while his deputy director, Jack Swaine, along with Scanlan, and Poliski sat quietly.

Krane shook his head, muttered something inaudible, and sat back in his chair. He then ran his hands over his face and sat forward.

'How many people have seen this?' Krane asked.

'Just the people in this room, and Randy Benson, the field office chief in Vegas.' Jack Swaine told him. 'Agents Poliski and Scanlan found the drive and showed it Benson who sent them straight to you.'

'Did you speak to Benson?' Krane asked.

'I just got off the phone with him. He's on full lockdown with it,' Swaine said.

Krane viewed the two Vegas agents. The pair lowered their eyes. Being stared at by the Director was not a thing they were accustomed to.

'Okay, here's how it is,' Krane began. 'This data could bring down the entire United States government and threaten our democratic process. I've only had five minutes with it, and I already know it's dynamite.'

Krane looked back at the laptop and shook his head, then focused on his deputy.

'Jack, I am placing you in charge of security for this,' Krane told him. 'Everyone who has seen this or knows of its existence is sequestered, to remain in one secure location, starting from right now. You are all being given the highest-level directive, by my office, to not communicate with anyone about its existence. You will surrender all your electronic devices to Deputy Swaine before you leave this room.'

Krane stood up and buttoned his suit jacket.

'Get these people to the secure company suite and make sure they are well catered for. Then get back here ASAP.'

He viewed his dismayed agents.

'Look, guys. My trust in your discretion is watertight,' Krane told them. 'However, the physical security procedures for a national threat of this magnitude have no wriggle room. This is the way it must be.'

He nodded once and left the room.

'Okay people, you heard the man. Give me your phones, then we're going for a little drive,' Swaine told them.

Tokyo, Japan

The grey, dark morning offered a continuous stream of rain as Ange made her way from her room at the Hyatt Regency to the Hilton where the boys were about to hold a press conference. Once in the hotel, she made her way to the Kiku ballroom.

Ange had arrived in Tokyo two days before the scheduled press conference. She longed to see the boys again, but she was there for a very specific reason. Going anywhere near the boys at this time would have been counterproductive. Yet it drove her crazy that the boys were just two blocks away and she had to wait to see them.

Ange kept herself busy. She created a fake press pass and dramatically changed her appearance.

At a top hair salon nearby, she had her hair dyed jet-black and cut into a pageboy. She looked at her appearance and giggled. She looked like an Asian William Tell.

'All I need is a bow and arrow,' she told her stylist, but the joke was lost on her. Ange bought two outfits of black leggings with matching waistcoats. One black and the other marine blue. She completed her ensemble with a pair of short heeled black riding boots, and basic silver jewellery. To complete her disguise, she found large trendy sunglasses and an umbrella with a lucky cat screen printed on it.

With her new look being almost local, Ange viewed the people in the conference room. One person she failed to notice was the red-haired western female posing as a news producer for MSNBC.

Ange had seen the woman, though nothing about her stood out, so she continued scoping the room, hunting for anyone out of place. Anyone who may offer a potential threat to her boys.

She knew the CIA was humiliated by their failure to prevent the free energy machine from being released to the public. Their failure extended to the fallout from Don Theck's taped confession on election rigging and media corruption.

Now the FBI had a detailed financial ledger on where the money went. How much money was paid, and who received it. The American President was on Twitter and Fox News screaming night and day about being framed and calling out fake news.

But at the end of the day, it was the CIA who failed the President and that will be very hard for them to live with.

She also rationalized that the CIA gained nothing from pursuing the matter further now that the machine was built and demonstrated to the world.

Nothing could stop the technology now. Ange's only concern was bruised CIA pride, and where that can lead.

Ange turned around again and saw the red-haired MSNBC woman was gone. She scanned the room and assumed she was out for a break. But that didn't make sense; the press conference was about to start.

Ange changed positions and scanned the room twice more. The woman was not there.

She decided to check the foyer. As she exited the conference room, Ange felt a presence behind her.

'Don't turn around,' a female voice told her. 'Take a left into the bathrooms.'

Oh, fuck! Ange thought. An American accent. She knew her options were limited, so she complied.

When she reached the bathrooms, she stopped. The woman poked her in the back with a round blunt object and ordered her into the disabled toilet room. Ange knew it was a gun, so she stepped inside.

She walked into the room, followed by the other woman. Ange knew this was her moment. She spun around and threw a roundhouse kick in direction of her assailant, attempting to hit both the woman and shift her gun position.

The red-haired woman was ready for her. She ducked under the kick and hit Ange hard in the chest, sending her backward.

Ange jumped to her feet, ready to charge, but the red-haired woman was no amateur. Her gun was levelled at Ange's face.

'Hi there,' the woman said. 'I am CIA Agent Rene Zeist. You must be the enigmatic Angelina Cohen, I presume.'

The White House

'Mr Haines will see you now,' the Chief of Staff's secretary announced.

'Follow me, please.'

FBI Director Lew Krane followed the woman into the office of Rolf Haines. As Krane entered the office Haines stood and welcomed him.

'And to what do I owe this little surprise?' Haines asked him. 'We don't have a meeting scheduled until next week.'

'Yes, sir, this was not on the books,' Krane told him in a voice that left Haines cold.

Haines called for his secretary to close the door.

'What's happened?' he asked Krane.

'It's big and I'm not sure it's politically survivable,' Krane said.

'Let me decide what's survivable,' Haines retorted. 'Your job is to spill the beans.'

'I'd rather just show you,' Krane said and took out his laptop, placing it on the desk facing Haines.

Haines sat and read the spreadsheets. He viewed the columns that described volumes of cash, bank accounts, and people. He snapped the cover shut and sat quietly for a full minute.

'Tell me everything,' he told Krane.

Ten minutes later, the two men were in the Oval Office. The President was having "study time", which was a euphemism for him watching Fox News repeats.

Fifteen more minutes passed before the President arrived.

'Sit, everyone,' the President told them. 'Did you see how Nick Hammer discredited the video of that Theck asshole? My God, he really did a number on him.'

'Don Theck is dead, sir,' Haines remined him. 'Please stop attacking the man on Twitter. It only makes…'

'When I want your fucking advice, I'll give it to you!' the President yelled. 'Now why the fuck have you interrupted my personal time?'

'On top of the Theck confessional video, that now has reached over five hundred million views, the FBI has found a ledger,' Haines told him.

'Of course, there's a fucking ledger!' the President yelled. 'There's always a fucking ledger!'

'The terrorists left the ledger at the Theck murder scene and it details cash payments to all our friends in the electronic media and social media, along with payoffs to Republican election officials.'

The President glanced at the numbers on Lew Krane's laptop for a few minutes, interrogated Krane for another minute, then threw a glass pitcher of water across the room.

'You know,' the President began, 'if you people had done your jobs, and I mean your job in protecting the President, this would never have happened.'

'My job is not to protect the President, sir,' Krane remined him. 'My job is to protect the…'

'You fucking idiot!' the President yelled at him. 'Get the fuck out of my office!'

Krane stared at this mockery of a President for a second, knowing what he had to do next.

'Leave the laptop, please,' Haines told him.

Krane had pre-empted this. The laptop was an office generic with nothing else on it except the spreadsheet.

He stood and gave a sickly smile at his President, nodded once, and left the building.

Men like Lew Krane didn't get into the positions they held in the world without knowing which media people they could trust. He also knew there was a tiny window of time in which to act before a net was thrown over him.

He took out his burner cell phone and dialled Mike Western of the *New York Post*.

'Where are you right now?' Krane asked him.

'In the office,' Western told him.

'Meet me at Chisels in fifteen minutes. Get ready for some bad weather.'

'How bad?'

'Category five.'

Western kicked back his chair and grabbed his coat. *Category five, hey. This should be fun,* he mused.

Tokyo Hilton

'We both know that if I wanted to kill you, it would have happened already,' Rene Zeist said flatly.

Angelina Cohen was seated on the toilet with her fingers laced on top of her head. She judged Zeist was too far away to launch a successful strike, so she relaxed and went along with the ride.

Death meant nothing to Angelina Cohen. She had died, in one form or another, several times in her life.

The emotion she was feeling, though, was curiosity. What did Zeist want, if not to kill her?

There was something about the woman's face. She had an aura of sadness about her, or was it guilt?

'I am going to lower my gun now,' Rene told her. 'It will do you no good to attack me, until I tell you why I'm here.'

Ange released her fingers and slowly opened her palms toward Zeist in the surrender position.

Zeist, in turn, slowly lowered her gun. The two women watched each other for a few seconds, then Zeist holstered her gun and closed her jacket.

'Let's get the fuck out of this toilet,' Rene suggested. 'I need a drink.'

The two women found a table in the back of the nearest bar. A waiter appeared within seconds.

'Two martinis,' Rene ordered. 'Dirty, no olives.'

'Wow!' Ange was impressed. 'You know my stress drink. How long have you been tracking me?'

'What? How the fuck should I know what you drink?' Rene winked at her. 'I wish we could smoke in here.'

Ange could not help herself from starting to like this girl. She acted like a redhaired version of herself.

Rene Zeist had done a lot of research before grabbing Angelina Cohen. She knew that Ange was a killer and if Rene confessed to being in the CIA ops room when the Japanese lab was bombed, Ange would likely kill her out of spite.

She also assumed Ange would accept that she was the manhunt lead, and therefore just doing her job.

So, that's what she revealed. She told Ange everything, right up to the actual bombing.

Ange listened to her story and evaluated how she told it. She listened for lies and omissions, but detected none.

'The million-dollar question is why are you here now?' Ange asked. 'Why are you telling me all this?'

Zeist threw back the dregs of her martini and enjoyed a soft belch.

'Why is it only men who think belching is fun?' Rene mused. 'I love to belch, and to fart.'

Ange smiled a genuine smile at her. In fact, she almost laughed.

'You're stalling,' Ange said mildly.

Rene Zeist shook her head and rubbed her face with her hands. She'd been awake for thirty-six hours and was exhausted.

'Okay. Here goes,' Rene levelled her eyes toward Ange. 'I've had a rough ride since the… you know…'

'The bombing,' Ange helped her out.

'Yeah, the bombing. The whole event caught me by surprise. One minute I'm tracking and hunting people my government said were terrorists. Then, boom! In a flash of light thirty people are dead.'

'Including Mackenzie James, my lover,' Ange added.

Rene nodded and looked away.

Ange placed herself in Rene's shoes. She had been where Zeist was many times. Working the case. Hunting the bad guys, until when the final moment of physical interdiction, and all that remained was blood and broken bodies.

'What a fucked-up life we both live,' Ange mused.

'I knew that if I didn't find you and apologize, I'd never sleep again,' Rene said. 'My sin was I never questioned if you were actually the bad guys. I blindly obeyed my orders; fuelled by ambition and deliberate ignorance. I'm no better than those fucking Nazi soldiers in the 1940s.'

She pushed her chair back and lowered her head.

'I think I'm going to be sick,' she said.

'Drink some water,' Ange told her. 'Then, we'll get some food before you puke all over that nice suit.'

That made Rene Zeist laugh, and it was not a happy sound.

The White House

Immediately following the FBI Lew Krane meeting, the President called his old crime gang of loyalists. The one or two good people in the President's circle marvelled at his ability to attract some of the worst people ever born in the United States.

These people were liars, cheats, and some were far worse. Their entire agenda was to tear America apart and rebuild it in their image. A cabal of fascists that would milk America dry.

Within a year or two, they would all be serving prison sentences. Each of them falling on their swords to protect their evil lord.

'Mr President,' Brian Zeal began, 'I believe the financial spreadsheet will leak.'

'You're a fucking genius, Brian,' the President yelled. 'Of course, it will leak. The fucking FBI would have leaked it already! They're traitors, did you know that? Traitors! I said they'd try to screw me as soon as I won the election. You heard me say it! Over and over; the FBI can't be trusted and now here we go. I'll bet they created this whole thing. They knew Don Theck and I were close. They knew it! And they used him to get to me! ME! I'm fucking

President. I'll tell you another thing; if this was Russia, or the Philippines, or Brazil, right now, I'd be able to put them all in jail! Those fucking FBI traitors. I mean, what the fuck has happened to this country? Past Presidents didn't have to endure this. The FBI worked for them, not the other way round. Why do they hate me so much? And it's not just the FBI, look at our corrupt media. I mean, by God, they think I'm some kind of punching bag...'

The President's people were used to his long rants of persecution. They knew it was a waste of time to try reeling him back in. So, they sat and pretended to listen. They made all the right sounds, and nodded their heads, until Mary-Jane Malone spotted her opening.

'Mr President,' Malone said. 'I have seen the video a dozen times, and it seems to me that Don Theck was drunk. Now I can't stop asking myself the question; was he just drunk, or did he also have a gambling problem?'

Her words resonated with the President, enough to stop him mid-rant. Having the natural born instincts of a ghetto rat, he knew instantly where this was heading.

'That's right, Mr President,' Brian Zeal added. 'Mary-Jane hit the nail on the head. And we know where there's a gambling addiction; there's also organized crime. Was Don Theck threatened by the mafia to make this video admission?'

'Mr President.' Mary-Jane Malone took the baton. 'If the video was staged, then the spreadsheet must be a fabrication!'

'I love it,' the President said. 'It explains everything. I knew from the minute I met Don Theck; he was a drunk, and a criminal. I want you all to spin it up for me and get it on Fox News, ASAP.'

Chisels Bar, Three Miles Away

Lew Krane and Mike Western reached the bar at the same time. They got a seat in the back and Krane showed his friend the payoff spreadsheet.

Western read the numbers and where all the money went.

'This is great,' Western said. 'But I got a call on the way here from my guy in the White House. They're already spinning it, and guess what? Don Theck comes out the bad guy.'

Krane laughed a sick little laugh.

'If this President shot an unarmed man in the street,' Krane said, 'Mary-Jane Malone would have Fox declare it was self-defence.'

'You know you'll never tag this guy, don't you?' Western said. 'I love that you try, but you are up against liars who have no boundaries. They have no souls, and they're not afraid of the law. They don't even bother weaving one element of truth into the spin. How can you compete against that?'

Lew Krane knew his friend was right. He was trapped in a government that was fully corrupt; that operated beyond the laws of man and God. Somehow, if he survived this job, he would just have to wait out the President's term, then hope like all hell the voters kicked him out of office.

Tokyo Hilton

In the bar, Ange and Rene ordered some light meals of tempura seafood, beef and vegetables. They both ate with relish.

At the end of the meal, they swapped phone numbers and made plans to meet again.

'I don't know why,' Ange told her 'But I have a strong feeling that you and I are not finished yet.'

Rene Zeist looked at this strong, beautiful woman. She too felt a connection that needed to be explored.

'I have to go and meet my boys,' Ange told her. 'Do you know if anyone from the CIA will come after them?'

'No,' Rene said firmly. 'That ship sailed the minute they demonstrated the machine. There's a lot of bad blood over there right now between the CIA and the government. A lot of nervous people, all focused on saving their own necks.'

'You'll contact me if anything changes?' Ange asked.

'I will,' she said. 'Call me before you leave Tokyo. I want to see you again.' Ange gave her a small smile.

'We'll have a girl's night,' she said warmly, then collected her things and made her way back to the conference room.

As the press conference came to close, Ange made her way toward the front of the room where the boys were seated in front of the cameras. She could clearly see their faces. They looked a little older and very tired after their long adventure.

Ange waited and watched until the final question was asked and answered, then the boys and their press managers got up and started to leave.

Ange followed them until a security officer stopped her.

'Sorry, ma'am. No press past this point.'

'I am Lucas Harding's sister,' Ange told him.

Ange handed the officer her card. It simply read Angelina Cohen.

'Please give this to him for me. It's very important.'

She watched the officer go after the boys. He returned with Lucas by his side.

The pair locked eyes, and Lucas's face lit up. His smile beamed from ear to ear.

'It's really you!' he called in a broken voice, then grabbed and hugged her so tight Ange couldn't breathe.

'We missed you so much,' he whispered in her ear. 'We talk about you all the time.'

'I'm so sorry I couldn't see you before now,' Ange told him. 'I had some loose ends to tidy up.'

'So I saw.' Lucas smiled at her.

She pushed him back and held him out at arm's length.

'Let me get a good look at you,' she said. 'Are they feeding you? You look a little thin.'

Lucas laughed.

'Same old Ange!' He laughed again. 'Always looking after me! You have to come up to our room. They've given us a really swanky suite.'

'I'll bet they did,' she laughed, knowing it was safe to join them now.

The pair chatted all the way out to the hall where the other boys were waiting. Another round of hugs and greetings followed, then they all rode the elevator high up into the hotel.

'I think we're going to need some room service,' Ange suggested. The boys cheered in agreement.

The end.